(IT ACCIDENTALLY FAMOUS

Books by David Baddiel

ANIMALCOLM

BIRTHDAY BOY

(THE BOY WHO GOT) ACCIDENTALLY FAMOUS

FUTURE FRIEND

HEAD KID

THE PARENT AGENCY

THE PERSON CONTROLLER

THE TAYLOR TURBOCHASER

(THE BOY WHO GOT) ACCIDENTALLY FAMOUS

DAVID BADDIEL

Illustrated by Steven Lenton

HarperCollins *Children's Books*

First published in the United Kingdom by
HarperCollins *Children's Books* in 2021
Published in this edition in 2022
HarperCollins *Children's Books* is a division of HarperCollins*Publishers* Ltd,
1 London Bridge Street
London SE1 9GF

www.harpercollins.co.uk

HarperCollinsPublishers
1st Floor, Watermarque Building, Ringsend Road
Dublin 4, Ireland

2

isbn 978–0–00–833427–7

David Baddiel and Steven Lenton assert the moral right
to be identified as the author of the work.
A CIP catalogue record for this title is available from the British Library.

Typeset in ITC Novarese Book 12/22pt
Printed and bound in the UK using 100% renewable electricity
at CPI Group (UK) Ltd

MIX
Paper from
responsible sources
FSC C007454

For Suz Gautier-Smith

CHAPTER 1
★ ORDINARY ★

Billy Smith was ordinary. He was *really* ordinary. For a start, he was called Billy Smith. It couldn't have been a more ordinary name. Unless maybe it was his dad's name, which was *John Smith*.

But Billy, an eleven-year-old boy, wasn't the only ordinary one in his family. Everyone in his family was ordinary. His parents were perfectly nice people with perfectly nice jobs, and Billy loved them, but there was no getting round the ordinary thing. His dad worked in an office. He was a clerk. Billy didn't really know what that meant, but his dad never explained it to him as what it actually involved was just too un-exciting. Too, let's face it, ordinary.

His mum – *Jane Smith* – was a manager at a packing company. Billy wasn't entirely sure what they packed. Some sort of fish. Frozen fish. Or maybe just fish, in general. Once again, she had the good grace to know that talking in depth about her career was not going to set her son's pulse racing. Which was why he remained unsure of the exact temperature or type of fish her company packaged.

Billy's mum wasn't actually working at the moment, though, because she had a baby to look after. Billy's ten-month-old sister, Lisa. You might expect her to be ordinary too. And you'd be right. To be fair, it's quite hard for babies to be out of the ordinary. Babies-wise, in non-ordinary life, there's Jack-Jack in *The Incredibles*, and Boss Baby in *Boss Baby*. Two. That's not very many:

most of the time, even on film and TV, babies just lie around, cry, eat, poo and wee. Which frankly are the *most ordinary* things human beings can do.

Billy was ordinary in every other way too. He wasn't top of his class, or bottom. He wasn't very good at sport, or very bad at it either. He wasn't popular or

unpopular: he had two really good friends, named Bo and Rinor, and went to a very ordinary school called Bracket Wood . . . OK – full disclosure (which may not be that much of a disclosure to anyone who's read any of my previous books). Actually, while Bracket Wood *was* a very ordinary school indeed, some of the pupils were not so ordinary. Or, at least, some not-very-ordinary stuff had happened to them. A lot of magical, or at least semi-magical, things seemed to have gone on in the lives of other pupils. Which, from Billy's point of view, made it worse. Because, although he had heard tell of all these extraordinary experiences (even if he was never sure whether to believe them or not), the school didn't feel at all extraordinary.

Certainly *his* life there didn't. Because nothing like that had ever happened to him.

And then something did happen to Billy Smith. Something extraordinary.

CHAPTER 2
TOTALTV TV

'**R**ight! Everybody! Please be quiet!' said Dan.

Dan was a man in his thirties, who wore a T-shirt with a logo on it from a very famous 1980s science-fiction film.

Billy, who was sitting in the middle of the Bracket Wood assembly hall, remembered his dad had begun showing that film to him once, and he'd tried to like it so his dad would be pleased, but it was really long and he'd fallen asleep.

'YES! EVERYONE! BE QUIET! OR ELSE!' said Mr Carter. 'I DON'T WANT TO HEAR ANY TALKING FOR THE REST OF THIS MORNING.'

'Um . . . actually, Mr Carter,' said Dan, going up to him and speaking quietly, 'that might be a problem. We *want* to hear the pupils talking. We're going to do interviews with some of them for a start.'

Mr Carter looked cross. 'But you told them to be quiet. So I was making sure they were quiet. I'm the head teacher and they do what I say.'

'I know. But I only wanted them to be quiet for a *bit*, long enough for me to explain what we were going to do. Not for the whole morning.'

Mr Carter thought about this for a second. Then he turned to the school, who were looking up at him from the Bracket Wood assembly hall.

'BE QUIET. FOR NOW, I MEANT!' He glared at them. And then threw in an: 'OR ELSE!'

Mr Carter nodded at Dan, meaning: *Job done!*,

and went to sit at the back of the stage.

Dan smiled a thank-you smile at him, and turned to the children, who were sitting and looking up at him expectantly.

'OK, thanks, everyone. So, I'm Dan. I'm a director. Of documentaries, for TV. And as you – and your parents, who have been sent letters – should all know by now, our company, **TOTALTV** TV—'

'Pardon?' said Mr Barrington, another teacher who was sitting at the back of the stage. Mr Barrington was quite old – no one at Bracket Wood was entirely sure how old – and wore very thick lenses in his glasses.

'**TOTALTV** TV.'

'It sounded like you said "TV" twice.'

'I did. The company is called **TOTALTV** TV.'

Mr Barrington continued to look confused.

'Anyway, yes,' Dan continued, 'our company is making a show called *School Daze*, and—'

'Sorry, pardon?'

Dan looked round again.

'Yes, Mr Barrington?'

'It sounded like you said "Days" with a Z.'

Dan blinked. 'I did.'

Mr Barrington smiled and frowned at the same time. 'Well, you're a little old to be in my English class, Dan, but you definitely don't spell "Days" with a Z.'

'IT'S A PUN, BARRINGTON!' said Mr Carter.

'Is it?'

'YES. ON "DAZE" AND "DAYS"!'

Mr Barrington blinked. 'Sorry, Headmaster, but didn't you just say the word "days" twice?'

'OH MY DAZE,' said Mr Carter. 'DAN. JUST CARRY ON. IGNORE HIM! IGNORE ANYTHING HE SAYS FROM NOW ON!'

'Right,' said Dan. He turned back to the children. Some of them had started talking among themselves during this bit.

'SHUT UP!' shouted Mr Carter.

They shut up.

'Um. Yeah. So we're making a TV show called *School Daze*. About life in an ordinary school! So all we need you to do is . . . be yourselves!'

All the teachers looked a bit worried when he said this. Dan continued:

'Just carry on going to your lessons and to games, and going out in the playground during break and everything, and forget about the cameras!'

'Headmaster,' whispered Mr Barrington, 'why are we doing this again?'

'Look around you, Barrington,' Mr Carter whispered back.

Mr Barrington did. 'Um . . . as you may know, Headmaster, my eyesight isn't very good. What am I meant to be looking at, exactly?'

'Oh my days. What you might notice, if you could see anything out of those glasses from 1973, Barrington, is that all the windows are cracked, all the floorboards are splintered, and all the radiators are broken. Beyond this hall, in the classrooms, you might observe that we do not have enough whiteboards, or computers, or even chairs. The school is almost completely broke. But TOTALTV TV have promised us a large donation for the privilege of filming here. So stop interrupting and just try and help them along, please! Or else you, my friend, will be looking at a new job at Geary Road.'

Geary Road was a school nearby which had an even worse reputation than Bracket Wood's.

Mr Barrington went white.

'But at Geary Road,' he said, 'they have a machine at the gate that checks for weapons!'

'Yes,' said Mr Carter. 'And if you don't have one, they give you one. For your own safety!'

While they were whispering, another man had walked on to the stage. He was dressed more smartly than Dan, although not in a suit. He wore a very soft-looking blue V-neck jumper, and very tight, uncomfortable-looking jeans. He was older than Dan, but his hair for some reason was much blacker. It sat on his head like a big black brick. He made a small hand-wave gesture towards Dan, who moved aside immediately to let him speak.

The man smiled at the children. His teeth were so white that a number of the pupils put their hands up to shield their eyes.

'*Hiiiiiii,*' he said. It was a very breathy 'Hi'. It seemed to go on for some time. As did the smile. 'I'm Stuart,' he said eventually.

There was another long pause. No one seemed to quite know what to say. Eventually, Mr Carter shouted from the back of the stage:

'SAY, "HELLO, STUART!"'

'Hello . . . Stuart . . .' said the school, although less together than writing it that way would suggest.

'Thanks,' said Stuart, smiling again. 'So, on this show, I'm what's called . . . The Producer.' (I've added capital letters here because the way Stuart said 'the producer' felt like they should have them.) 'I'm, let's face it . . .' he continued, adding a little chuckle, 'the boss. I mean, I own TOTALTV TV. Totally. So. Y'know. The buck stops –' he pointed to himself – 'here.' He looked out and smiled again, possibly expecting laughs. There weren't any. He carried on smiling. 'And *School Daze* . . .' He raised a finger without turning round, towards Mr Barrington behind him. 'With a Z! Is my idea. My baby, if you will. And I've chosen to give my baby –' he put both his palms out, towards the children, as if he was giving them a very special invisible gift – 'to you.'

'Seems like it's the other way round!' shouted a child's voice from the back of the room. Billy, and most of the rest of the children, turned round. It was the naughtiest boy in the school: Ryan Ward.

Stuart looked out at the crowd of kids, putting a hand up (palm down, fingers straight) to his – quite bushy – eyebrows, as if that might help him see across this distance. The gesture wasn't necessary as it was only about thirty feet.

'Sorry?' he said, his smile refusing to fade.

'Well, you want to make a documentary about school. So you need a school. You need us. Which makes *us*, I would say, *our* gift –' Ryan held both his palms out in front like Stuart had done, mirroring him – 'to you.'

'RYAN WARD!' shouted Mr Carter. 'I THOUGHT YOU'D STOPPED BEING NAUGHTY SINCE . . . ANYWAY, I THOUGHT YOU'D STOPPED!'

'Please,' said Stuart, his smile now starting to look like a very white force field. 'It's no problem. So, some of you are a bit feisty. Great! Our viewers will love that!' He looked back out across the hall. 'And, hey: maybe as *School Daze* goes out, and becomes the big, big hit I think we all know it's going to be, one of *you* out there . . .'

He pointed a finger, out into the crowd. It moved along the width of the hall.

Then it stopped. It seemed to be pointing directly at . . . Billy Smith. A few children looked round at him.

' . . . is gonna become a *star*,' finished Stuart.

There was a pause. Stuart continued to point towards Billy. But Billy just shrugged. The children who had looked round at him laughed.

Because, although it might be true that one of the kids at Bracket Wood was going to become famous because of this TV show, Billy – and everyone else – knew it *wasn't* going to be him.

CHAPTER 3
MINDY AND MANDY!

It's not that Billy didn't like the idea of fame. As with most children, perhaps most people, it seemed to Billy that these days being famous was the most desirable state of being to . . . be. He thought being famous just seemed amazingly great and cool. He sometimes even stole his mum's magazines, most of which were about famous people (and their marriages and haircuts and diets), and devoured them from cover to cover, wondering how fantastic it would be to be *in* them, rather than just read them.

He liked the idea. Of course he did. He just knew it wasn't anything that was ever going to happen to him. At break, after the announcement about *School Daze*, all the Bracket Wood kids ran excitedly out into the playground. The cameras had already started shooting. Billy looked around. He could see that Barry Bennett and his friends were doing football tricks for them. Elsewhere, Ryan Ward was making a whole group of his friends laugh, probably with jokes about the teachers. All over the playground, Billy could see the friendship groups forming, and playing up in different ways to Stuart and Dan, who were standing behind the camerawoman, pointing and instructing. He could see the camera move and turn, taking in the entire scene.

The camera never seemed to be settling on him for any length of time.

After standing watching everyone else for a bit,

Billy was joined by his two best friends, Rinor, who was a boy, and Bo, who was not, even though her name was nearly 'boy'. Billy and Rinor and Bo had their own little friendship group. It didn't cross over at all with any of the other ones at Bracket Wood.

'Hey, Billy,' said Bo. 'This is exciting, isn't it?'

Billy nodded.

'Stuart – is that his name? – the one with the teeth like from an American advert – he said *any* of us could be a star . . .'

'Yes,' said Billy.

'Wow. I'd love to be known all over the world!' said Rinor.' And not just in Balmadömölk!'

Balmadömölk was the town in another country very far away where Rinor's grandparents lived.

'Are you well known in Balmadömölk?' said Billy.

'By my nan, yes.'

'That's not many people.'

'She has fifteen brothers and sisters. They all

know me as well.' He frowned. 'Actually, Great-Uncle Erag has never been quite sure who I am.'

'OK.'

'I'd like to have my own YouTube channel.' said Bo.

'I can really imagine that,' said Billy. 'You'd be great on it!'

Bo blushed a little. Billy liked Bo very much. She had been nice to him from the first day she arrived

at the school, when they were in Year Two. Little six-year-old Billy had been too shy to make any friends then, but Bo just came up to him where he sat in the corner of the classroom not speaking to anyone, stuck her hand out and said, 'Hi, I'm Bo! I like sour sweets, fat furry cats and Pixar films. What's your name?' They had been best friends ever since.

'What would you do on your channel?' asked Rinor.

As Bo thought about this, out of the corner of his eye, Billy noticed, leaning against the school wall, one of the teachers, Miss Gerard. Miss Gerard, who often came in late and fell asleep in lessons and sometimes had very black teeth, was, he noticed, reading *Yeah!* He recognised it from the front cover because *Yeah!* was one of the magazines about famous people that his mum – and, secretly, he – liked to read. Every so often, Miss Gerard glanced up, as if she was listening in on their chat, but Billy didn't imagine that a grown-up, a teacher, would be interested enough in what he and his friends talked about at break to do that.

'I'd talk about Pixar films and things,' said Bo.

'Great!' said Billy.

'What would *you* do, Billy?' said Rinor.

'I don't know,' said Billy. 'I just can't imagine anyone wanting to watch *me*!'

'Yes, they would!' said Bo.

'Who?' said Billy, laughing.

Bo and Rinor both paused to think about this. But, before they could answer, Miss Gerard suddenly appeared at the edge of their circle and said:

'I don't know if any of you three know this, but being famous – it normally . . . well, it *used to* require a little something called *talent*.'

'Pardon, miss?' said Billy.

'Well, in my day—'

'When *was* that, miss?' said Bo.

'Don't be rude, Bo.'

Bo looked innocent, as if she hadn't been, but then again Bo was quite good at looking innocent when she hadn't been.

'In my day, as I say,' continued Miss Gerard, 'you had to be able to sing, or dance, or tell jokes, or write books, or . . . I dunno: do *something*. You couldn't just *be* famous. For nothing. Like . . . what's she called . . . Sunny Tomato?'

'Do you mean . . . ?' said Billy.

'This one,' she said, opening her copy of *Yeah!* and unfolding two pages to show a teenage girl, about seventeen years old, with long blonde hair and loads of make-up, standing, in one photo, on a beach, looking out to sea dreamily, and, in another, with deep-red hair, dressed in a leather jacket and sticking her tongue out to camera.

'Sunshine De Marto!' said Bo. 'Oh, I just *love* her!'

'Yeah, she's cool,' agreed Rinor. 'I just love her too.'

'Yes, I know. You all do,' said Miss Gerard. 'But *why*? What does she do that makes her loveable and cool?'

Bo shrugged. 'I just like her hair. The way she changes the colour of it every time she goes out. In every photo! And all her make-up tips! And her Chiwaapoos!'

'Oh!' said Rinor. 'Mindy and Mandy!'

'OMG. *Sooo* cute! Did you see when she dressed them up like nuns?'

'Amazing.'

'I hate to ask what Chiwaapoos are, but I feel I have to,' said Miss Gerard.

'It's a Chihuahua and poodle crossbreed, miss,'

said Bo. 'She's got two of them. Mindy and . . .'

'Mandy, yes. Got it.'

The bell for the end of break rang. Miss Gerard shook her head and did an 'in you go' wave at the children. They set off back towards the school building. After the other two had gone, Miss Gerard put out a hand to stop Billy.

'What about you, Billy?'

'Pardon, miss?'

'You didn't say anything.' She unfolded the magazine again. There was Sunshine De Marto, looking out to sea. There she was, sticking out her tongue.

'I'm trying to hold out a little beacon of hope, but . . .' said Miss Gerard, 'I assume you're the same – I assume, like the others, you think Sunny Tomato is really cool?'

Billy looked at her. He could tell she wanted him to say, *No, miss, I'm not very bothered with her*. Or, *No, miss, actually I'm more interested in books, or maths, or classical music*, or something else that grown-ups thought was important. But he just said: 'Sorry, miss, I have to go to class now.' And rushed in.

Because the truth was that Billy Smith *was* bothered with Sunshine De Marto.

Secretly, Billy Smith was a Sunshine De Marto *superfan*.

CHAPTER 4
MAYBE ANOTHER TIME

OK, 'superfan' implies something a bit crazy. Which Billy was not. To be clear: Billy didn't have a special room in his house covered in pictures of Sunshine. He didn't practise speaking like her in the mirror. And he never considered that, when he got older, he might get a tattoo of her face somewhere on his body.

But he *did* think she was cool, and he sometimes thought it would be amazing to meet her. Which he never would, of course. Someone like Billy –

someone so ordinary – would never, he knew, get to meet Sunshine de Marto.

He could read about her, though. So when he got home that day he did immediately go into the living room to see if his mum had bought the new edition of *Yeah!*

She had. It was there, lying on an armchair. He picked it up and flicked quickly through to the pages that Miss Gerard had waved at him, the ones with Sunshine on them.

'Billy?'

He looked up. It was his mum, holding his baby sister, who was asleep on her shoulder. Billy went a bit red, and shut the copy of *Yeah!* because he didn't know if it was OK for him to look at her magazines. Sensing this, she said:

'Don't worry, I don't mind you looking at my silly mag. It's just the usual pics of famouses being famous. I don't know why I bother!' She suddenly yawned, quite loudly.

'Are you OK?' said Billy.

'Yes, fine. Just a bit tired.' She nodded towards the baby. 'This one kept me up all night.'

Billy nodded. 'Why don't you leave her down here for a bit? I'll look after her. And you can go upstairs and have a nap?'

His mum smiled. 'Maybe I will in a bit. Thank you! How was school?'

'It was OK. Oh, those TV people came in and started filming.'

She frowned. 'Oh, yes. We had a letter about that that we had to sign, didn't we?' She looked at him with concern. 'Were you OK about it? It didn't make you feel nervous or anything?'

Billy shook his head. 'No! It's fine. They'll just film all the other, more interesting, kids, I expect.'

His mum came over and sat down next to him. She put the sleeping baby down on some cushions in front of her. She touched his shoulder.

'Billy. You shouldn't do yourself down so much.'

Billy smiled. 'What do you mean?'

'You shouldn't think people won't be interested in you! Why wouldn't they be?'

Billy shrugged. 'Because there's nothing interesting about me?'

Jane put her hand on his shoulder. 'That's not true, Billy. It really isn't.'

'You would say that,' said Billy. 'You're my mum!'

'Yes,' said Jane. 'That's true. But so is the fact that you're much more unusual than you think. For a start, most eleven-year-old boys wouldn't offer to look after the baby so their mum could have a nap.'

'Who's having a nap?' said Billy's dad, coming through the front door. He spoke far too loudly, as he sometimes did when he was a bit confused. Which meant that the baby woke up and started screaming.

'Oh dear,' said Jane. 'Maybe another time . . .'

CHAPTER 5
A TRUE THING HAPPENED TO ME ONCE

The next day, Billy's class had English, with Mr Barrington. Mr Barrington had asked everyone to write a story about something that had happened to them in real life. This was an ordinary thing for an English teacher at a primary school to do. What was less ordinary was that the *School Daze* production team had decided to begin their filming of lessons with this class. They had set up one of their cameras at the back of the classroom, and another at the front. Which made it feel not at all ordinary.

'Um . . .' said Mr Barrington, standing in front of the whiteboard. 'Shall I start the lesson now?'

He was looking over towards Stuart, who was standing with headphones on, looking at a small TV monitor that he was holding in his hands. In front of Stuart, Dan was whispering something to the camerawoman, who was called Natasha. She was nodding and slowly adjusting the lens.

'Pardon?' said Stuart.

'Fine to kick off now?' said Mr Barrington.

Stuart, still smiling, but not really with his eyes, took a deep breath.

'OK, Mr Biddletown—'

'Barrington.'

'Whatevs. As I think I made clear earlier, we just want everyone to carry on as normal. Just pretend we're not here—'

'That shouldn't be hard! He can't see you anyway!'

'Ryan Ward!' said Mr Barrington, turning round sharply. 'I may not have very good eyesight, but I certainly heard that!'

Stuart looked pleased. 'Did you get that?' he said to Natasha. 'What a great bit of naughty boy bantz!'

'Er . . . no, sorry,' said Natasha.

For the first time since he'd arrived at Bracket Wood, Stuart's smile fell. 'What?' he said angrily.

'Sorry, Stuart, but I stopped filming when the teacher asked if we were ready . . .'

Stuart stared at her, hard. He shook his head. 'You're a camerawoman, right?'

'Yes,' said Natasha, sounding very small.

'That means you film. You film until I—'

'Or I,' said Dan.

'Yes, but mainly I . . . tell you to stop. Is that clear?'

'Yes,' said Natasha, sounding even smaller. She pressed a button on the camera. On the side of it, a small red light appeared.

There was a long, awkward pause. Then Mr Barrington said:

'So . . . shall I start the lesson now?'

'YES!' shouted Stuart. He shut his eyes. Without opening them, he took a deep breath and seemed to . . . *restart* his smile. Then he opened his eyes. 'Sorry. Mr Barrelthwaite. Of course. Go ahead.'

Mr Barrington, not bothering to correct his name this time, nodded. 'So, class. Who wants to come up to the front to read their "A true thing that happened to me once" story first?'

A flurry of hands went up. Billy's – although no one noticed this – did not.

CHAPTER 6
★ RE-LATE-ABLE ★

'''**A**nd that was when I woke up at the vet's. All my family were there. And I wasn't a chinchilla any more. Nor was I a tortoise, or a pig, or a cat, or a monkey, or a pigeon, or any of the other animals I'd been changed into when I was on the farm or in the zoo! I was a boy again!'''

Malcolm Bailey looked up from his story.

Mr Barrington nodded. 'The end . . . ?' he said.

'Yes.'

'OK. Thank you, Malcolm . . . Do go and sit down.'

Malcolm did so. Mr Barrington frowned. He looked out at the entire class.

'To be honest, Year Six, I'm not sure any of you really understood what the assignment was. You were all meant to write a true story.'

'Yes, sir!' said the class. 'We know.'

'Well, I'm really not sure any of you did.' He looked round at the children. 'We've had Barry Bennett's story about going through his bedroom wall into a world where he could try out a whole series of new parents . . . Fred and Ellie Stone's was about being given a magic video-game controller that let them control people . . . In Sam Green's essay he wished for his birthday to happen every day, and then, apparently, it did! Ryan Ward wrote possibly the most absurd tale, about how he had *swapped bodies* with our head teacher, Mr Carter. And Rahul Agarwal – and really, Rahul, I think of you as normally quite a sensible boy – seems to have written a story about transforming Amy Taylor's wheelchair into a supercar, and then driving it to Scotland, and then, as if that wasn't enough, a whole other story about how that girl you brought in a little while ago, who I quite clearly remember was German, was actually from the year 3020! I mean, *honestly*!

Alfie Green's story started off perfectly straightforwardly, about spending an evening in with his babysitter, but by the end of it he was escaping from somewhere called –' Mr Barrington squinted down at some notes he had been taking – '*Farty Harbour!* With a talking dolphin. Called Dolph.'

He looked up and sighed. 'And now you, Malcolm Bennett, have regaled us with a tale about how on the last school trip to Orwell Farm, you were changed by a magical goat into a series of different animals . . .' He shook his head. 'I mean, I thought you didn't even like animals!'

'I didn't use to, sir. But now I do. In a way, it was that experience at the farm that taught me how to.'

'Right. Well. Good. But that's not really the point I'm making . . . Oh! Hello!'

He said this last part, because while he'd been talking, Stuart had approached him on one side. Mr Barrington, who as we know did not have great eyesight, hadn't noticed. But also Stuart seemed to glide, softly, rather than walk. Stuart put his arm round Mr Barrington – which Mr Barrington didn't seem at all comfortable with – and turned him away from the class.

'Mr Biddleton,' he whispered. 'We have a problem.'

'Are the cameras not working?'

'No . . . when I say *we*, I kind of mean *you*. All of you at this school.'

'Not quite with you, Stuart.'

'OK, Mr B, here's the thing about today's filming from our POV. One story told by one kid about their real life that sounds completely barmy . . . fine. That's great. That's a splash of colour. That, for the viewer, goes into the category of "crazy kidz" . . .'

'With a Z?'

'Yes. But . . . all of them? That's weird. This is meant to be a documentary about ordinary kids in an ordinary school. Like, today, I want to hear an ordinary, relatable story from an ordinary, relatable child. And if Bracket Wood aren't going to be giving us that – well, I don't quite know what TOTALTV TV are doing here. And maybe we should go somewhere else. Which would be a shame. Wouldn't it?'

He looked very closely at the teacher when he said this. Which was an impressive thing to do, as Mr Barrington's lenses were so thick his eyes up close looked like monstrous jellyfish. If Stuart could have seen through them, though, into the other man's mind, he'd have seen only a memory, from the assembly the day before, of Mr Carter reminding Mr Barrington about the large donation that TOTALTV TV had promised to the school. And the words: *'Help them along, please! Or else!'*

Mr Barrington gulped and nodded. Stuart smiled even more widely, turned the teacher back round to face the class and glided back to camera.

'One word, Mr B,' he said, when he got there. 'Three syllables. Re-late-able. *Re-late-able.*'

'Um . . . that's *four* sylla—' Mr Barrington looked at Stuart. 'Never mind. So. Yes. Ahem. OK. Does anyone want to read out one more essay? And do please remember the title is "A TRUE – that's TRUE – Thing That Happened To Me Once".' He gazed out despairingly at Bracket Wood's Year Six. He peered along the rows of desks. Most of the children had already read out their stories. Through his double-thick lenses, though, he could just make out that a hand, one single hand, had gone up.

He squinted hard.

'Oh . . . Billy, is it? Billy Smith?'

'Yes, Mr Barrington.'

Mr Barrington took a deep breath. 'OK, Billy. Come to the front and read your story.'

Billy also took a deep breath, and got up.

CHAPTER 7
IS THAT THE END?

What with the cameras being there, and everyone else's stories being so amazing, Billy hadn't been at all sure about volunteering. His hand had gone up slowly, and nervously. But this might be his only chance to have any kind of moment on camera. He felt it was now or never.

He stood at the front of the class, holding his exercise book, with his story written neatly in it on the lined paper. He looked round at the camera. Dan was just staring blankly at him. Stuart was smiling at him, but Billy had learned by now that Stuart just smiled all the time, whether he was pleased, furious or, as he seemed now, impatient. The only person who was looking at him with genuine niceness was Natasha, the camerawoman. She smiled at him, and did a little nod, which seemed to mean: *Off you go! Don't worry!*

Billy turned back to the class, cleared his throat, and began reading.

"'Once, last summer, we went to a theme park. Except we didn't actually make it. We got half the way there, and then my baby sister did a big sick on my dad's trousers, so we had to turn back.'" He looked up. He hadn't written the next bit down, but felt he should add: 'I mean, it was really a lot of baby sick, and my dad didn't have a spare pair of trousers, and he couldn't go on the roller coaster in his pants.' No one in the classroom said anything in response to this, so he looked back down at his book. "'Then, another time, for my birthday, we were supposed to go to my favourite burger place, but there isn't one near where we live, so we went to one which was supposed to be a bit like it, called Five Boys. Except when we got there it was a clothes shop, for boys aged five.'"

Billy had thought this bit of his story might get a laugh. It didn't. It got tumbleweed (this is a comedian's word for the sound of no laughter). He sighed to himself (just in case you're not clear, it's the sound of weed tumbling across a windy wasteland) and continued:

"'One day, we went to see my grandpa. He lives in another town. When we got there, he'd forgotten to buy teabags, so my mum said to me, 'Billy, can you go and get some from the shop?' That was unusual because I don't normally go out and get stuff from shops. My parents do that. Especially

because this was a shop I'd never been to before. Although, when I got there, it was really like all the shops I had been to before.'" He looked up. He noticed that quite a lot of the children had started looking out of the window. Some were doodling. Gunther Flackle had fallen asleep.

"'So I bought the teabags, and then I had enough money left over for some crisps. I bought my favourite, sweet chili flavour. Hot stuff!'"

He looked up again. He had imagined that saying 'Hot stuff!' would really go down well. He had imagined wrong. A not particularly nice girl called Isla Fawcett sniggered, but in a way that seemed like she was laughing at him, rather than with him.

'Anyway . . .' he continued. '"The last thing I thought I would mention for this essay is that, two weeks ago, my mum and dad said that for my birthday we could buy a kitten.'"

A few heads in the room turned round at that.

One of the doodlers stopped doodling. Gunther Flackle grunted, although stayed asleep.

'"Me and my mum and dad spent ages looking for one on the internet. We found a pet shop near us, and on their website was a black-and-white one that looked perfect. We decided to call him Furrballs."'

This actually did get a ripple of appreciation from the room. Someone said 'Ha! *Furrballs* . . .'

I'm on a roll, thought Billy.

'"So we all went to the shop, and yes, there was Furrballs, in a little cage! With his six brothers and sisters, all different colours."'

Most of the class was now listening. Even Mr Barrington was nodding and stroking his chin.

I've got them eating out of my hand, thought Billy.

'"The pet shop owner got the little kitten out very carefully and handed him to my dad. Then my dad gave Furrballs to my mum. Then, finally, she handed him to me. He looked up at me with his little green eyes. I thought, *This is definitely the kitten for me!*"'

Everyone, now, was rapt.

'"And then I sneezed. Really badly. Again and again and again. Big loud sneezes. They only stopped when they took Furrballs away from me. It turns out I'm allergic to cats."'

He looked up. Everyone in the class frowned and glanced at each other.

'So . . .' said Isla Fawcett, eventually, 'you *didn't* get a kitten . . .'

'No. I'm allergic to them.'

'Right,' said Isla. 'Well. I wouldn't open with it.'

Billy didn't really understand what this meant. He looked around. Everyone looked very disappointed. Billy closed his exercise book.

'Um,' said Mr Barrington. 'Is that the end of your story?'

'Yes,' said Billy.

'Well. Good. Thank you very much, Billy.'

Billy nodded, and went to sit on his chair. He looked down at his desk. He heard Mr Barrington say to Stuart – it was meant to be a whisper, but the class was so quiet it was more than audible – 'Was that . . . "everyday" enough for you?'

'Oh, *yeah*,' said Stuart. 'Maybe too much.'

Billy sighed. He felt a bit sad and a bit stupid.

CHAPTER 8
IT IS ME, DAD

The filming of *School Daze* went on for quite a while. Billy's story was the only time he was aware of being filmed by the cameras. He noticed them at lunch, at break, and a few times they came back into his class, but they never seemed to focus on him. The other boys and girls who had told their amazing stories continued to capture all the attention. So Billy assumed that, when the show went out, his bit wouldn't even be in it.

He looked forward to the programme being shown, anyway. It was still exciting to have his school on the telly.

The first episode went out on a Thursday night at 8.30 p.m. He and his parents sat down to watch it after their normal dinner of fish fingers, chips and peas. Actually, to be fair, it wasn't the Smiths' *completely* normal dinner. Billy had asked if they could have something a bit special to celebrate, what with it being the first episode of *School Daze* that night. So his mum had added two triangular slices of bread and margarine to each plate.

The TV programme started. To a soundtrack of some bouncy music, it had an opening sequence which showed lots of children Billy knew. In fact, it showed almost everyone in his class – Barry, Fred and Ellie, Alfie, Bo and Rinor – all of them. They and some of the younger children from the school were running around, or reading, or doing PE, or walking through the corridors, or sitting cross-legged in assembly. What none of them were . . . was him.

Then it began. A voice-over said:

'Your school days. Good or bad, you never forget them. The child, they say, is father – or mother – to the man – or woman. Well, on this programme we shall find out how true that is!'

'What does that mean?' said John.

'Shh!' said Jane, nodding to the baby, asleep in a little basket at her feet, but stirring. 'Use your inside voice.'

'Well,' said John, 'I don't get it. How can a child be a father to a man?'

'Oh, for heaven's sake!' said Jane. 'It's like you've never heard of anything!' This was undoubtedly true about Billy's dad: he did seem not to have heard of very much. 'It's a saying!'

'It means,' said Billy, 'that what you're like when you're young can tell someone a lot about what you're going to be like when you're older.'

John looked confused. 'Well, it should be "the child is a lot like the man", then.'

'Shh!' said Jane again. They looked back to the TV. It was cutting between various children being interviewed. 'Yes, I like it here!' Ellie Stone was saying. 'It's a good school!' said Malcolm Bailey. 'It's all right,' said Ryan Ward, 'if you're happy to end up on the scrapheap.' But then he smiled, to let the cameras know it was just a joke.

Then it cut to Mr Carter, in his office, saying:

'Yes, well, when I took on this school, I knew it would be a challenge . . .'

'Are you going to be in it, Billy?' asked his mum.

'I don't know, Mum.'

His mum frowned. 'Well . . . did they film you saying anything?'

'Yes. Once. A little bit. But I don't know if they're going to use it.'

'I'm worried, frankly . . .' This was the TV again. Miss Gerard was speaking to a girl who Billy didn't know, a girl in Year Four. The teacher was clearly, Billy thought, aware of the camera. Firstly, it was the morning, and her teeth weren't black. Secondly, she was putting on a much posher voice than normal. And, thirdly, she was pretending to be concerned about the child. ' . . . that if your work doesn't improve, I may have to speak to your parents!' The girl looked at her, a bit confused, as if she too had never seen Miss Gerard like this.

'Are there any more fish fingers, Mum?' This was Billy's dad, who called Billy's mum 'Mum' too.

'I'll go and have a look in the freezer, Dad.' This was Billy's mum, who, yes, called Billy's dad 'Dad'.

With this, it was clear to Billy that his parents had lost interest in the show. He felt relieved. He hadn't liked that they were expecting there to be a lot of him in it, when he knew that they were going to be disappointed. But as well as relieved he also felt a bit sad. Even though he'd known he wouldn't be in it much, he had hoped that somehow *School Daze was* going to make him famous.

That seemed less and less likely as time went on. Everyone else was in a lot of the shots. There was even a bit with Rinor and Bo in the playground, talking about what they liked to do at break, which went like this:

BO: I like to stand here with my friends, talking.
RINOR: I like to think about lunch.
BO: What, even when I'm talking to you?
RINOR: (after some thought) Yes.

Billy thought he had been with them that breaktime, but then realised that he was just out of shot of the camera, on the other side of Bo.

Then, with about ten minutes to go before the

programme ended, it cut to his classroom, and Mr Barrington was saying: 'So, class. Who wants to come up to the front to read their "A true thing that happened to me once" story first?'

'Mum! Dad!' shouted Billy. Both of them had gone into other rooms. 'I think I might be in this bit!'

His mum came rushing back in, his dad a bit more slowly. On the telly, lots of the children put their hands up. The voice-over said:

'One thing that perhaps is a bit of a problem at Bracket Wood is what the word "true" means. As you're going to find out . . .'

This was followed by a montage of the children in his class reading their essays. It didn't show all of them, but it showed enough to allow viewers to see that a lot of amazing stuff seemed to have happened to the kids in Year Six. Or, because the voice-over kept saying things in between the readings like *'You thought that was wild? Hold your horses for the next one!'*

and *'There's still more crazy young imagination to come!'*, the programme kept suggesting that the kids were *making up* a lot of amazing stuff.

Then the voice-over said: *'Does no one in this class live anything like a normal life? Oh, wait . . .'*

And then, on the screen, Billy stood up.

'Oh my goodness, Billy!' said his mum.

'Wow!' said his dad. 'It really looks like you.'

'That's because it *is* me, Dad.'

Billy felt very nervous. Which was strange, as he wasn't about to do anything nerve-racking. He was just going to watch himself. But, still, he had terrible butterflies in his tummy.

'Once, last summer, we went to a theme park,' Billy (the one on the telly, that is) began. 'Except we didn't actually make it . . .'

As his reading went on, the camera cut away a lot, to show other pupils looking . . . well, there's no other word for it: bored. Fred Stone yawned. Sam

Green looked out of the window. Ryan Ward made a silly face. Even Rahul Agarwal, who was probably the cleverest and politest boy in the class, had stopped listening and started doodling numbers and shapes in his book.

Billy had not noticed all of this happening at the time, when he had been reading his story. Now, though, he felt hurt and upset. A tear started to come into his eye.

'Oh, Billy . . .' said his mum, and she rushed over to put her arm round him.

'It's OK,' he said, brushing the tear away. 'I guess it *is* a pretty boring story.'

'No!' said his dad. 'It was great!'

'Well, that's obviously not what anyone else in the class thought,' Billy said quietly.

'I'm sure that's not . . .' said his mum, turning back to the telly, where, unfortunately, Mr Barrington's eyes – very large behind his thick lenses as we know, and even larger on the TV screen – were closing. ' . . . true,' she said anyway, because she always tried her best to be a good mum.

'They seem to be giving your story the longest time, though,' said his dad, who also tried his best, parenting-wise.

'That's because they're trying to make it clear how boring it was,' Billy said.

John Smith opened his mouth to reply, and then realised that Billy was probably right. So they just had to sit there in silence, as Billy's story seemed to go on and on. Eventually, he got to the bit about not getting a kitten. And then the bit where Isla Fawcett said:

'Well. I wouldn't open with it.'

The voice-over added: *'In case you don't know what*

that means, Isla is saying to Billy: "If you ever find yourself on stage telling jokes and stories to an audience, don't start your routine with that one!"'

Then there was the bit where Mr Barrington said, 'Is that the end of your story?' and the bit where Billy said, 'Yes.'

'*So . . .'* said the voice-over, as Billy went back to his desk and sat down, 'that *was exciting. We can only hope that, one day, Billy writes a sequel!'*

The family stared at the screen.

'Well,' said Billy's dad. '*He* liked it, at least.'

CHAPTER 9
#RELATABILL

As soon as the show ended, Billy went to bed, earlier than usual.

As he got to the bottom of the stairs, he saw an older copy of *Yeah!* that his mum had left on the table by the landline phone, the one that only rang these days when cold callers were trying to sell his parents new types of heating or broadband. In the magazine, there were photos of Sunshine again, but these were different from the usual ones. These were of her with her mum and dad in the house she grew up in. It was a small house, that looked a bit like the one Billy lived in. Her mum and dad looked really ordinary as well. *She* still looked amazing, of course, but in the interview she talked a lot about how, even though she was a superstar now, she was just the same person she had always been, and that her favourite thing was going back and visiting her parents and her old friends in her old neighbourhood.

'I think what my journey proves is that anyone like me can be a superstar!' she said, which was the second time she used the word. 'It doesn't matter where you come from. Chase your dreams! Otherwise, they might never come true!'

When he'd first read these words, Billy had found them exciting. He'd seen them and thought, *Yes, she's right. I do want to be famous, so I should try and do something about it*. Fame always felt a long way away; it felt like a country that people like him weren't allowed to go to, but sometimes when he read an article about Sunshine and she said those things, he thought: *Maybe even I could get there.*

But tonight had made it clear: he couldn't. Fame was never going to be for him, or anyone like him. He would never be famous, and he would never get to meet Sunshine De Marto.

In fact, tonight, he just wanted to go to bed and never think about being famous or meeting Sunshine De Marto ever again. Tonight, it wasn't just the idea that *other* people might think his admiration of her a stupid thing. *He* thought it was a stupid thing. *He* thought it was stupid, imagining himself ever being in the same space, on the same page, as her. And unusually for Billy, who was a very gentle soul, he threw down the copy of *Yeah!* on the floor quite hard (admittedly, throwing a glossy magazine on the floor isn't going to be a *very* violent thing to do, no matter how hard you do it). Then he turned to go upstairs.

Suddenly, his mum appeared in the hallway.

'Billy?'

'Hi.'

'Are you OK?'

'Yes,' he said quietly.

'I'm so annoyed with that TV company—'

'Please, Mum. I don't want to talk about it.'

She nodded, but looked very sad. Suddenly, her phone rang. She took it out of her pocket and looked at it.

'Oh! It's Bo's mum.'

'Really?'

'Hello, Lin? Oh! Hi, Bo . . . um . . . yes, he's here. He's already in bed, though . . .'

Billy reached out a hand for the phone. His mum shrugged and handed it over.

'Hello?' said Billy.

'Hey, superstar!' said Bo.

'Pardon?'

'I'm talking to you, hashtag boy!'

'OK, Bo. I'm going to say "Pardon" again.'

'Hashtag BillyTheNormo. Hashtag OrdinaryBilly. Hashtag – and this is the one that's really trending – Hashtag Relatabill.'

'Relatabill?'

'It's a mash-up of your name – well, Bill, which kind of *is* Billy, isn't it? – and the word "relatable": Relatabill!'

'Yes, I get that. *Where have you seen that?*'

'Oh. My older sister says it's all over Instagram. And my mum says it's on Twitter as well. Even my gran rang and said it's on The Facebook. That's what she calls it, The Facebook . . .'

Billy frowned. 'Sorry, I still don't quite see what this has to do with me.'

Bo tutted. '*You* are BillyTheNormo. *You* are OrdinaryBilly. *You* are Relatabill!'

'I am?'

'People loved you on that show! They loved you because you were the only one in our class to tell an ordinary story! That felt – well – relatable!' Billy heard a shuffling noise on the other end of the line. 'OMG!'

'What?'

'OMG twice. Now my sister says there's a TikTok version of it!'

'Of what? I didn't do a dance or anything . . .'

'No, but . . . Oh, she's bringing it over . . . Oh, go and have a look . . . ! It's amazing!'

CHAPTER 10

471,250

Billy did. He wasn't allowed to have a phone, but obviously his mum did (the one they'd been speaking on). What she didn't have was TikTok. So it took a little while, with his mum saying, a lot, 'It's called what?' and 'Oh, I see, like a *clock*,' before she actually managed to download it.

Then, of course, she spent a long time trying to search for the video that Bo had been talking about before Billy saw – and was amazed to see – his face, right there, on the front page of TikTok. *It was one of the trending videos! The #Relatabill Rap!*

'Mum!' said Billy. 'Click on that one!'

'Why?'

'That's me!'

'Oh!' She clicked. It was Billy, reading his story. Only . . . it had been made . . . cool. Someone called **crazzclips64** had put what his mum, trying to sound younger than she was, called a 'banging' backing track behind Billy's words. They had then scratched and mixed all those words up so it sounded like Billy was repeating some and leaving out others:

'Once, last summer, we went to a theme park.

Except we didn't

We did

We didn't

We did

My baby sister did

A big sick

So we had to turn back

We had to turn

A big sick

On my dad's trousers

Into weeeeeeeeeeeee!'

It went on like that. As Billy spoke – as he rapped! – loads of graphics appeared on the screen, in time with what he was saying: lots of red and blue squiggles, a cartoon image of a baby being sick, and, for some reason, a white cat nodding its head in time with the music.

Billy liked it. It was silly but it was also kind of cool. But what was *really* cool was that when he clicked off the video, underneath the little heart symbol was the number '470K'.

'OMG, look, Mum!' said Billy, pointing to it.

'That's nice, darling. Four hundred and seventy likes. Who's K?'

'No, Mum. That means it's been liked four hundred and seventy *thousand* times! It's been liked by *four hundred and seventy thousand* people!'

Billy's mum frowned at the screen. 'Really?'

'Well, no. Now it's 471,250 people. It's going up all the time!'

Billy's mum looked closer at the phone. 'Oh dear. Is that OK?'

Billy thought this was a strange thing to say, but before he could answer, his dad appeared.

'Mum? Billy? I've got a weird email from Jeremy, who works in my office.'

John Smith always referred to his friends like this. Jeremy, Dave and Pete, 'who work in my office'. His other friends – Steve, another Dave and Mike – worked in 'the other office'.

'OK,' said Billy, who generally wasn't interested in emails from anyone who worked in either office.

'It's about you, Bill.'

'Is it?' said Billy.

'Yes. Look.'

He handed Billy a piece of paper. This was another thing Billy's dad did: rather than showing people stuff – like emails or things he'd seen on the internet – on his phone, he printed them out.

This particular email was quite badly printed out, as everything his dad printed out was. But Billy could make out a photo of himself reading out his essay on *School Daze*.

'Sorry, Dad – what is this?'

'Oh, hold on,' said Billy's dad. 'The stupid printer did it on two pages.'

He handed Billy another bit of paper. Which made it clear what it was: a newspaper article! It was from the website of a big newspaper that his dad always called *The Daily Tale*, which had already printed a review of *School Daze*.

There was a section of type his dad had highlighted in yellow. He did this quite a lot with things he printed out. He had got the yellow highlighter from 'the other office'. Billy read out loud:

The undoubted star of *School Daze* is a young boy in Year Six called Billy Smith. In these times when almost every young person seems to want to be famous, and perhaps has to pretend they already are by making things up, here at least was a boy prepared to just tell it how it is: my life is really boring.

He looked up.

'Sorry, Mum. Sorry, Dad. I didn't actually think that *was* what I was do—'

'Never mind about that, Billy,' said Jane. 'What else does it say?'

Billy looked down.

It was a joy to hear Billy tell his ordinary story of ordinary life, and ordinary mishap. Although his companions in the class seemed distinctly unimpressed, it brought tears to my eyes. Tears both of laughter, but also of compassion for this sweet young man and his humility. A famous writer once said that the job of the artist is 'to give the mundane its beautiful due'. Billy Smith did that on *School Daze*. Which makes him, too, an artist.

He looked up again. 'I don't really understand what "mundane" means.'

'I think it's just another word for ordinary,' said his dad. 'Look at the headline!'

Billy did so.

SCHOOL DAZE DAZZLED BY
AN ORDINARY BOY

And then, below that, underneath the photo of him, it said:

Star of school reality show Billy Smith reads his 'boring' essay.

'Star'. The word echoed in Billy's head.

Star.

CHAPTER 11

BILLY! BILLY!
BILLY! BILLY!

Next day at school, things were very different for Billy. Normally, he just arrived, said goodbye to his mum or dad, walked into the playground, spoke a bit to Bo and/or Rinor and went inside the building.

No one (apart from Bo and Rinor) paid any attention to him.

This time, he could feel, by contrast, that *everyone* was paying attention to him. *Everyone* was noticing him. It felt almost like the whole school had waited for him to get there, just to see him. In fact, it didn't just feel like it, it looked and sounded like it as well. As Billy approached the gates, he could hear lots of children shouting and screaming and running about in the playground as usual. But as soon as he came through the gates they all stopped. Everyone stood stock still. Everyone paused their shouting and running and turned to look at him. It was like a scene from an old cowboy film, when a dangerous gunslinger comes through the swing doors into a rowdy saloon bar.

Billy looked around. The random shape of people in the playground seemed to have somehow formed into a big triangle. On one side stood years One, Two and Three. On the other, years Four, Five and Six. And, at the far side, all the teachers. Billy walked through the middle of this triangle, towards a little gap at the top, where he could see the front doors of the main school building. Everyone just watched him, silently. Billy could feel multiple pairs of eyes on him. It was really, really *weird*.

Then, just before he went through the gap at the top, someone behind him shouted 'Billy!' He turned round. It was Bo, coming through the school gates, late. She was smiling at him, looking excited, looking like she really wanted to talk to him about what had happened. And Billy smiled back, because he really wanted to talk to her about it too.

But they never got a chance to, because suddenly everyone started shouting his name at once. It was like Bo shouting it had broken some kind of dam, and the next thing Billy knew, everyone in the playground was saying 'Billy! Billy! Billy! Billy!' and coming towards him really quickly.

'Billy! You're famous!'

'Billy! You're a star!'

'Billy! How does it feel?'

He could just about make out what people were saying. But everyone was crowding and jostling him. It was amazing, but it was also a bit frightening. Even Miss Gerard had bent down, right next to him, looking very excited, and was saying his name too. She was so close he could see that her teeth were not actually black but kind of grey.

'Billy! Can you sign my rough book?'

He turned round. It was Isla Fawcett! Isla Fawcett who was always pretty horrible to him, and had been so rude about his story. She was smiling at him and holding out her book at a blank page. In her other hand was a pen.

'Sign it!' she repeated.

'Sign what?' said Billy.

'My rough book!'

'But . . . what do I write?'

'Your name, of course!' said Isla. As she said it, she

laughed, and batted her eyelashes, and shook her long hair around her face in a strange way.

'Um . . .'

'Yes!' said another voice. 'Sign my book!'

'No, mine!'   'Sign my bag!'

'Sign my arm, Billy!'   **'Sign my leg!'**

Billy looked around. There were lots of pens and lots of people and lots of parts of people being held out towards him. He didn't know what to do. He looked to Bo, but she had now got pushed behind most of the people crowded in front of him. Billy heard her say, in a concerned voice:

'Billy? Are you OK?'

But before he could answer, he felt himself being pulled inside the school.

CHAPTER 12
AS A PERSONALITY

'So! Not-so-silly Billy! Diddy Biddy Baxter Willy William! Sir Billiam Of BillaBong!'

Billy nodded, a bit confused, as Stuart, who – despite the tightness of his trousers – was crouching down so his face was really close to Billy's, continued to say versions of his name.

He – Stuart – was smiling his biggest smile, and it felt as if his teeth, huge in Billy's vision, might chomp his head off. But that seemed unlikely, as, at the moment, Stuart seemed, as far as Billy could tell, very, very pleased with him.

'Or should I call you *Relatabill?*'

They were standing in the head teacher's, Mr Carter's, office. Mr Carter was there too, as were Miss Gerard, Mr Barrington and Dan the director.

They were all standing around a little awkwardly, watching Stuart and Billy.

'I think just . . . Billy would be best, Stuart, to be honest,' said Mr Carter. 'That is, after all, still his *name*.'

'OK, boss!' said Stuart. He held out his hands to grasp Billy's shoulders. 'Billy. Do you realise something?'

'Um . . . I don't know,' said Billy.

'Yes, wait till I've told you what it is. *You* are the big breakout star of our show. You, Billy Smith, are the kid from *School Daze* who *everyone* is talking about!'

Billy did kind of realise this. But he wasn't sure he was meant to say that, in case it ruined Stuart's moment. So he just said:

'Wow.'

'Yes. Wow indeed! You know what you did, Billy?'

'No.'

'Yes, just wait and let me tell you. It was another rhetorical question. I thought that was maybe clear from the last time.'

'Right, yes.'

'You gave the people – the viewers – what they wanted. Because they – like you – are Billys.'

'What's he talking about?' whispered Miss Gerard.

'It's rhyming slang,' Dan whispered back. 'Billys – Billy Bunters. For punters. That's what he calls . . . um . . . ordinary, not-famous people.'

'Yes,' continued Stuart, 'the Billys out there – never forget – they don't want to see too much craziness, or glamour, or out-of-the-ordinariness on TV! What they want to see up there on the screen is *themselves*! And last night they saw themselves big time! They saw their very own Billy!'

'Anyway, Stuart,' said Mr Carter. 'I think we – and indeed Billy – really have to get on with the school day.'

'In a moment, Mr C. First things first.'

'I think, for our students, starting the school day, Stuart, really *is* the first thing we need to do—'

Stuart, ignoring him, handed Billy a piece of paper. 'Do you know what this is?'

Billy looked at it. 'Is it a contract?'

'Yes,' said Stuart, a bit taken aback. 'Sorry, I thought you were going to say "no" and I was going to have to say "let me tell you" again. But, yes. It's a contract.'

Billy looked at the piece of paper. It had a lot of long words on it. Words like 'heretofore' and 'legally' and 'discretionary'. He looked up, at the teachers.

'I don't really understand this,' he said.

'Actually, Stuart,' said Mr Carter, 'I think perhaps we should let the school review this before anyone signs anything . . .'

Stuart looked up at the head teacher. 'Well, of course. If you *want* to hold up TOTALTV TV continuing to invest in your pupils, that's up to you, Mr Carter.'

Mr Carter blinked, said, 'Hmm . . .' and backed away, looking troubled.

'You don't have to worry too much about the small print,' said Stuart, returning his attention to Billy, who was still staring at the contract. He got up from his crouching position. He put his arm round Dan. 'What you mainly need to understand is that we –' he moved his finger very quickly between himself and Dan – 'at TOTALTV TV want to take you on. As a personality. As a *star*. We want to make sure that you get to squeeze all the juice out of this moment, Billy. We want to . . . *look after you*.'

'For money,' said a voice at the back of the room: a girl's voice. Everyone looked round. It was Bo. She was leaning against the back of the door.

CHAPTER 13
EXCLUSIVE WORLDWIDE REPRESENTATION

'**B**o . . .' said Mr Carter. 'When did you sneak in here?'

'Sorry, Mr Carter. I was just outside in the corridor and –' she looked at Billy – 'I was worried for my friend. And now I'm more worried. I'm worried that someone might be wanting to exploit my friend.' She turned away from Billy, towards Stuart. '*For money.*'

There was an awkward silence for a moment.

'Well,' said Stuart, moving towards her. 'That is

good of you to be concerned, Boo.'

'Bo. You're just getting it wrong deliberately now. Plus – by the way – I don't even think last night's episode was *meant* to show Billy in a good light. I think you were trying to humiliate him. Because you thought it would be funny. But then people liked him *anyway* . . . and so you've decided to go with that and see what more you can make out of it!'

Stuart – for the first time since his arrival at Bracket Wood – looked a bit uncomfortable. He shifted uneasily from foot to foot. But then he recovered himself, and did a dismissive wave at Bo. 'Whatevs. Point is. I think –' he turned to Billy – 'I think a *star* like Billy can make up his own mind. Can't you, Billy?'

'Er . . .' Billy wondered about this. He wasn't even very good at making up his mind about what to have for tea (although, luckily, that was normally fish fingers, chips and peas). So he really wasn't sure he could make a decision about something he knew very little about. Like – he looked at the contract again – 'exclusive worldwide representation'.

'I mean,' carried on Bo, 'who *else* do you "look after"? Anyone we might have heard of?'

'Ah,' said Stuart, looking very sure of himself with this one, 'I think you may have heard of . . .' He looked around the room, beaming. 'Jackie Noodle?'

Everyone looked very uncertain. Mr Carter shook his head. Miss Gerard shrugged.

'Oh, for heaven's sake,' said Stuart. 'Well. Um. Six Bananas!'

Again, everyone look stumped. Eventually, Mr Barrington said, 'I think we might be able to get you five . . . I could ask the dinner ladies?'

'Saints preserve us,' said Stuart. 'They're only the biggest boy band since Fast Charge!'

'Since . . . ?' said Mr Carter.

'You haven't heard of Fast Charge! OMG!' Stuart looked around him. 'Is this school on Mars?' he cried.

'I just think maybe there's a lot more famous people than there used to be,' said Miss Gerard. 'Not like in my day, when you knew who was who.'

Bo folded her arms, triumphantly. Stuart shook his head. And then Dan said:

'We do look after Sunshine De Marto . . . ?'

Everyone took a breath. Billy looked up at Dan, wide-eyed.

'Well, of course,' said Stuart. 'I mean . . . I hardly thought I had to mention *that* . . . I thought everyone already knew *that* . . .'

'Although Mindy and Mandy – the Chiwaapoos? – have their own agent,' said Dan. 'We have to negotiate separately for them to appear with her.'

'Do you really?' said Bo, unable not to look impressed.

'Sorry, who?' said Mr Carter.

'Sunshine Tomato!' said Miss Gerard. 'Come on, head grandpa!'

'I could get . . . to meet . . . Sunshine De Marto . . . ?' said Billy, quietly.

Stuart and Dan exchanged glances. 'Oh, that could easily happen,' said Stuart. He got a shiny black pen out of his jacket pocket and held it in front of Billy's face. 'In fact, I'm *sure* of it.'

Billy looked up at him. He could almost see Sunshine's face in Stuart's eyes. He reached out and grabbed the pen.

'Just one thing,' said Bo. 'Billy's eleven. I assume he can only sign a contract with his parents' permission.'

Stuart looked at her. His smile did that thing of staying fixed, but seeming not very much like a smile any more. He turned round to face the teachers.

'Sorry . . . should she really be in here?' he said.

'Not really,' said Mr Carter. 'But I think she's right about the parental permission, actually.'

Meanwhile, Billy suddenly saw another piece of paper appear in front of him. He looked up. It was being slid into his hands by Miss Gerard, who was smiling at him in a way he'd never seen before.

'Just one little autograph, please, Billy. If that's OK,' she said.

CHAPTER 14

WHAT'S THE WORST THAT CAN HAPPEN?

Bo *was* right. Billy couldn't sign the contract without the consent of his parents. That might have been a problem for Stuart. Which was perhaps why, later, after school, he decided to pay the Smiths a visit.

He stood in their living room, with the family all there, and said:

'No, I don't want any fish fingers, thank you, Jocelyn.'

'Jane. I can do them with or without peas?'

'Yup. Still no. So. Here's the thing. Your son – *Relatabill* here – has become so popular that we've decided to maybe add a little something to our broadcasting schedule.'

There was a pause here. Billy and his mum and dad looked at each other. Stuart stood with his arms

open, smiling at them. His smile seemed to have acquired sound: it was like it was loud.

'Sorry,' said Billy's dad. 'What have you . . . um . . . maybe decided to add to your broadcasting schedule?'

'I'm coming to that. Just leaving a bit of a dramatic pause.'

'Oh. OK.'

'Because it's quite something.'

'Right.'

Another pause. Another loud bit of smiling. Then, suddenly, he raised his voice:

'Dan! Nat!'

Through the living-room door – they must have been waiting in the hall – came Dan and Natasha. Natasha was holding her camera.

'I've spoken to the channel. And they have approved it. A spin-off show – *At Home with the Ordinarys!*'

'*At Home with the* . . .' said Jane.

'Yes, we wanted to just call it *The Smiths*, but apparently there was a band called that a hundred years ago or something. Plus, always good to let people know what they're getting.'

'Right,' said John.

'I mean, that's Billy's *brand*, you see,' Stuart pointed out. 'Ordinariness.'

'Bill's got a brand . . . ? Since . . . last night?'

'Oh, yes,' said Stuart. 'And one of the tent poles of that brand is going to be *At Home with the Ordinarys*. It'll be a reality show. Shot here. In your very own house.'

Jane and John and Billy looked at each other once again. 'What do we have to do?' said Jane.

'Nothing!' said Stuart. 'That's the key. Just . . . I don't know . . . What kind of things do you normally do?'

Jane and John and Billy looked at each other again.

'Watch telly,' said Billy.

'Eat fish fingers, chips and peas,' said John.

'Change the baby,' said Jane.

'Brilliant! You are the Ordinary kings! And queens, of course, Jess.'

'Jane.'

''Evs.'

'So . . .' said Billy. 'Just because people seemed to like me being . . . ordinary on *School Daze*, you think there should be another whole show about my family being ordinary?'

'Yes!'

'Won't people want something different now maybe? Now that they've *seen* me being ordinary?'

Stuart didn't just smile at that. He laughed. Billy hadn't seen that before. 'Ho-ho-ho!' he went, his teeth flashing very, very white. It was like Father Christmas had had a lot of cosmetic surgery to make him look much younger and more sleek.

'No, no, Bill,' Stuart said, when he'd stopped laughing. 'The way showbusiness works is: once you've had a hit – just do the same thing again. And again. And again. Call it something a bit else, or whatever, but basically just serve up the thing that worked before on a slightly different plate! That's what the Billys want!'

'Billys . . . ?' said John.

'Punters. As in Bunter,' said Billy.

'What?'

'Never mind. I don't really understand either.'

'So, what do you think, Smithsonians!' said Stuart.

'It's just Smith,' said Jane.

'I know that. I was just saying it in a zany way!'

'Oh, sorry, I thought it was you, um . . . getting the name wrong . . . again . . .'

'What do we think, Billy?' said John. 'You're the famous one. Do you think it'll be OK?'

My dad thinks I'm famous? thought Billy.

'Well . . .' he said. 'It's been fun so far!'

'All right!' said John. 'Let's go for it. What's the worst that can happen?'

Natasha coughed, quite loudly.

'Are you OK?' said Jane.

'Fine,' she said. 'Maybe just need some water.'

'You can have some in a minute,' said Stuart, handing John Smith the pen. 'First of all, I'd like you to get the family on camera, signing the contract . . .'

CHAPTER 15
DISGRUNTLED POSTAL WORKERS

On Monday, at school, things weren't much quieter for Billy. All the other pupils kept trying to get him to autograph their books or take selfies with him on their phones. Gunther Flackle even asked him to record a message to his dad, who Gunther said was 'Billy's biggest fan'. Eventually, the teachers decided to move Billy into a separate room.

To keep him company, Bo and Rinor were allowed in as well.

They sat round a desk with the official school laptop computer on it. This was an old machine from about 2007 with a tiny screen. Miss Gerard was standing at the back of the room, supervising, as children of their age were not allowed to look at online stuff unsupervised. She was no longer looking bored, though, as she might have been a few days ago, or cross with them about what they were interested in. Now, every time Billy looked up at her, she returned his look with a strange kind of watery smile.

Bo, Rinor and Billy were viewing another video mash-up of his storytelling on YouTube. This one had made it into a heavy-metal track, in which someone had autotuned Billy's voice so that he sang – well, he screamed – his essay, like:

Once, last summer, we went to a theeeeeeeeeeemmmeeee park!

Then loads of guitars and drums crashed in, and

the video went all cut-up and jerky to make it look like Billy, and everyone else in the classroom, was banging their heads in time to the music.

'I think I like this one more than the Relatabill Rap,' said Rinor.

'What? Don't be silly,' said Bo.

'We are big fans of heavy metal in Balmadömölk,' added Rinor. 'This song reminds me of our top group, Death Potato. They are the biggest band we have produced since Disgruntled Postal Workers.'

'Right,' said Bo. 'Of course. So anyway, Billy . . . did you sign it? The contract?'

'Yes,' said Billy. 'Sorry.'

'Hey,' said Bo. 'It's up to you. I'm sure it's the right thing to do. What did your mum and dad say?'

'Well, they signed it as well.'

'Really?' said Rinor.

'Yes. TOTALTV TV are doing a spin-off show set in our house.'

Bo looked at him. 'Wow.'

'Yeah.'

'You really *are* going to be famous.'

Billy looked at her, and then back at the screen. 'Well. I think I kind of already am.'

Bo frowned. This was the first time since this had all started that she thought Billy had said something that didn't sound very like him.

'I mean, this is so cool,' he continued. 'This video. And look at all the comments. All my fans.'

He clicked on the bottom of the screen. There were hundreds of them.

'All your *what* now?' said Bo.

'Well, they are, Bo. Look. "I love Relatabill!" he said, reading the first one. "Billy Smith is the best!" "Go, Billy!" "#BillySmithForPrimeMinister!"

Bo looked at him. He was entranced by these messages, she could see that. She looked back at the screen. She was a very fast reader, and scanned down them quickly. Then she said, pointing out of the window:

'Hey, look over there!'

Billy looked out of the window. 'What?'

'There's a pigeon walking in a funny way.'

'Where?'

'Oh, it's flown away.'

Billy looked back. The screen had gone blank.

'What's happened?'

'Oh,' said Bo. 'I guess this ancient computer must have gone down again . . .'

'Hmm,' said Billy. 'It *is* rubbish.'

'It's still better than the one we have in Balmadömölk,' said Rinor. 'Everyone shares it.'

'You have one computer in the whole of Balmadömölk?' said Billy.

'Yes. Everyone in the town gets to use it for half a day every year. But my family, because we are important, also get use of it at Christmas. Which in

Balmadömölk is of course on May the seventh.'

Bo watched them talk, pleased that Rinor's Balmadömölk stories were distracting Billy. It meant that he wouldn't notice that she had stuffed the computer charging lead into her pocket, just like he'd already not noticed that she'd quickly unplugged it while he was looking out of the window.

Which meant – which was why Bo had done it – that now he wouldn't notice that at the bottom of those online messages had been one that said:

'I hate Billy Smith. He's so stupid and ugly and boring. And he SHOULDN'T be famous. #cancelBilly.'

CHAPTER 16
SOCKS!

The next few weeks were a whirlwind. *School Daze* continued to go out on TV, but Stuart told Billy that they'd 'recut it according to the new brand focus'. Then, after he'd said it again and Billy still looked confused, he said: 'We're going to have more of *you* in it than before.'

Since Billy hadn't done much else except read out his story in class that time, this meant that future episodes of the show had a lot of him sitting at his desk, eating his lunch, standing around in the playground and occasionally saying 'oh'. But even that seemed to work well, in terms of his, as he called them now, fans. Because people online said things like – and Billy read this one out to Bo and Rinor too – 'I just love how Billy Smith does, like, nothing on *School Daze*. That's exactly what I was like at school! All the other kids are such try-hards!'

Meanwhile, TOTALTV TV began shooting *At Home with the Ordinarys*. At first, the Smiths, despite what Stuart had told them, thought they needed to *do* stuff. Especially John, who, it turned out, had as a child wanted to be a magician, and saw *AHWTO*, as Stuart called it, as his opportunity to fulfil that dream.

Which meant that during the first bit of filming (of the family having tea, of fish fingers, chips and peas), he made the brown sauce bottle disappear. He put a tea towel over it, said 'Hey presto!' and when he took it off it was gone. The rest of the family applauded, but, following a signal from Stuart, Dan shouted: 'Cut!'

'What's wrong?' said John.

Stuart came over, smiling of course. 'Yes. John. It is John, isn't it?'

'Yes.'

'Where's the brown sauce?'

'Well now. That would be telling. A magician never gives away his secrets.'

'It's in your trousers, isn't it?'

'Urrgh, Dad!' said Billy, looking under the table. The top of the brown-sauce bottle was indeed poking out of the waistband of John's trousers. 'I'm not using any of that sauce now.'

'John,' continued Stuart. 'Good trick. Great trick. But magic – that's not the point of *At Home with the Ordinarys* . . .'

'It's not?'

'No. If anything, the opposite. You're on here, the Smiths, because the one thing you're not, as a family, is magical.'

With that, Stuart walked back behind the camera. And after that, the camera crew for *At Home with the Ordinarys* shot the Smith family doing literally what they did every day, which was really not very much.

But while *AHWTO* was being made *School Daze* was still on the TV. Billy's fame just seemed to grow and grow – and, with it, Billy's need to track his fame. He spent a lot of time on the internet, googling himself. Luckily for Billy, so far he hadn't come across anyone posting anything like Bo had seen at school. In fact, he discovered a whole load of fan sites dedicated to him: BillySmithIsMyHero.com. BillySmithStans.com. And of course Relatabill.com (although that one had been set up and trademarked by TOTALTV TV). On these sites, people posted mainly how much they loved to watch Billy on *School Daze*, but also information about Billy. *Wrong* information. But Billy liked that too.

'This post says that I'm really an adult disguised as a child!' he read out over the phone to Bo. 'And this one that I'm actually a member of the Royal Family, sent to Bracket Wood under cover by MI6.'

'To do what?' said Bo.

Billy looked. 'It doesn't say.'

'Right.'

'Oh, this one says that in real life I'm really, really unusual and exciting, and I only pretend to be boring and ordinary for the cameras.'

Right, thought Bo, wanting to say, *I think maybe, Billy, since you've been on camera and got much less ordinary, you might have actually got MORE boring*, but she bit her tongue.

Billy also spent a long time working on his signature. He'd decided that, if he was going to be famous, he should have a proper one, for autographs. In the early days, when he'd signed for the people who were asking him to at school, he'd just written out his name, and he noticed that it was a bit different every time. Sometimes it had a big round B and two little Ls, and other times a thin B and massive Ls. And the Y only occasionally looked like a Y; sometimes it looked like an M or an N.

I need to make this the same all the time, he thought. *To fit in with my, as Stuart says, 'brand'.*

He tried this:

But then he thought that that looked a bit too jolly. If this was a famous person's signature, it might be a professional clown. So then he tried:

But that looked too young. It looked like the Hairy Caterpillar.

His third attempt just involved underlining it too much and, in fact, accidentally crossing it out:

He was about to give up, but then a letter arrived at his house. It was a letter the likes of which none of the Smiths had ever seen. Not even the contents: just the envelope. It was gold – shiny gold – and seemed to be made of paper so thick you could, in an emergency, *wear* it. Perhaps as some sort of scarf.

'Is it from Willy Wonka?' said Jane, handing it to Billy. This was a bit of a tricky manoeuvre because she was walking around with Lisa over her shoulder, burping her.

'No, Mum,' said Billy.

'I know it isn't really, Billy.'

'Oh. Shall I open it?'

'Well,' said John, 'it is addressed to you.'

Billy nodded. He felt the envelope was so swanky it seemed a shame to tear it, but nevertheless, with a view to keeping it somewhere later as a treasure, he carefully threaded his finger under the flap and ripped it along the top. He took out the contents, which was a piece of card, again luxuriously thick, on which was written an invitation. To him. And his name had been handwritten in ink by someone on it.

It said:

TOTALPR PR REQUEST
THE PLEASURE OF
Billy Smith
FOR THE PREMIERE OF
THE NEW PIXAR MOVIE
SOCKS!

'Wow!' said Billy.

'*Socks?*' said John.

'It's the new Pixar movie! About the secret life of laundry!'

'Oh!'

'Oh goodness, Billy,' said his mum, 'A *premiere* . . .'

Billy was very excited about it. Even the word sounded incredibly glamorous and important: '*premiere*', like somewhere where everybody who was there was the *first* of everything. He couldn't wait to tell Bo, who loved Pixar films, and Rinor, who insisted that the opening scenes of *Wall-E* were based on everyday life in Balmadömölk.

But Billy's eye was also caught by his name on the invitation. That was it. *That* was how he should sign his name. It was an ordinary signature for an ordinary guy, but whoever wrote it had playfully turned the dots above the Is into little circles, making it just a tiny bit different. *A tiny bit more like a signature*, Billy thought, *that someone famous would have.*

So he copied it – first with tracing paper, and then freehand – until he got it perfect: until it became *his* signature.

Which meant that when he arrived on the red carpet at the premiere for *Socks!*, he would be ready.

CHAPTER 17
THE MONTAGE SEQUENCE

Soon after this, fame began to make Billy's life *really* exciting (and not a little weird). Because, soon after the invitation to the premiere, he got invited to loads *more* amazing events!

'Goodness,' said his mum, sorting through all the post that had started arriving for him every day. 'You're getting invited to everything, Billy!'

'Yes,' said his dad. 'And in the old days you

often weren't even invited to your classmates' birthday parties.'

'John!'

'What?'

'That's not a nice thing to say!'

But Billy laughed, because it was true. A tiny part of him looked forward to getting an invite, this year, to Isla Fawcett's birthday, and being able to say, 'So sorry, Isla, I can't make it this year, unlike last year when you didn't invite me – not sure why that was. Maybe because you thought I was really boring and not famous then? Anyway, I can't make it because on that day I may be going to . . .'

Well, there were quite a few options there. He could tell Isla he couldn't make it because he was going to:

A fashion show

Billy wasn't just invited to the show, he was invited to appear in it! Unfortunately, Billy hadn't realised this – he thought he'd just be watching –so had turned up in his normal T-shirt and jeans. The people running the show really liked this – 'Crazy! Ironic! So ordinary it's "out there"!' they said. But then, at the last minute – 'just to add a bit of pizzazz!' – they decided to give him some enormous roller skates to wear with it. It was really fun, zooming down the runway on them, while lots of people clapped and took photos!

A posh restaurant

Stuart took Billy, his parents and baby Lisa (who didn't eat anything except milk from a bottle) to a place called *Pie* to celebrate his new-found stardom. It doesn't sound posh, a place called *Pie*, but Stuart explained, to blank looks from Billy and his parents, that this was part of what was posh about it. In fact, all the food on the menu sounded not that different from what Billy would have at home. They even had fish fingers, chips and peas! Only, when it arrived, the fish fingers were made out of raw fish, and the peas out of what the waiter called 'freshly sourced seaweed caviar'. Unfortunately, this

124

meant that as soon as the waiter was gone, John Smith said, 'I feel sick,' and Stuart said, 'Oh, for heaven's sake, I suppose you'd prefer Burger Munch across the road.' The whole family glanced at each other and said: 'Yes!' And so it was that they ended up leaving Pie to have a lovely slap-up fast-food lunch at Burger Munch.

A visit to a spiritual guru

This was someone who, according to TOTALTV TV, was going to help Billy feel more like a star. Stuart was concerned that Billy wasn't quite confident enough in himself, and although (as Stuart told Billy's mum and dad) that 'fits great with the Relatabill brand' he felt that it would be no bad thing if Billy had a tiny bit more self-belief, now that he was (again, Stuart's words) 'living the dream'. 'He still seems sometimes a little . . . *scared* by fame. We don't want that. Plus,' he added, 'it's a fab photo opportunity.'

So Billy and his parents and the baby went – with Natasha, taking photos – to the house of Astral, the guru, who was a bald man with a very long beard. Jane put Lisa in a travel cot as she was crying a lot, which Astral looked slightly cross about.

The guru sat crossed-legged on a mat, surrounded by candles. He seemed to be wearing only a blanket, which was troubling for Billy, but he put it out of his mind. Eastern music was playing. Astral told Billy (and Jane and John) to lie down on the ground, and close their eyes, and just – and he said this

with a lot of emphasis – *breathe*. Billy did that. Astral said, very slowly, in a voice that was itself very breathy, 'Breathe in . . . and out. Breathe in . . . and out.' Which Billy thought was a bit strange as he did know how to do it. In fact, it always, in his experience, just kind of happened.

The words 'Breathe in . . .' (with Astral's voice going up) 'and out . . .' (with Astral's voice going down) carried on for a while. Soon, as Billy had been worried might happen, his mum and dad began to snore. Even the baby had stopped crying and fallen asleep. But Astral didn't seem to mind and just carried on giving the breathing instructions. Finally, after what seemed like ages, he added some other stuff, like:

'Believe in yourself . . .'

And:

'Don't care what others are saying about you.'

And:

'You have the power within you. You can do anything!'

And:

'Ridicule is nothing to be scared of.'

Which Billy felt he'd heard somewhere before, on an old song his dad liked, but by then he was nearly asleep himself, so he forgot about it.

'Wow,' said Billy's mum when they woke up. 'That's the longest nap the baby has ever had! Can I hire you to come to our house and do that again, Astral?'

'Nope,' said Astral, in a noticeably less breathy voice.

A TV appearance

Billy was booked to be on a kids' TV show called *In Yer Face!*, on a channel called EStuff Junior. He sat on a big pink square – not a chair, a big pink square, made out of chair material – opposite the presenters, also on big pink squares, who were called Jez and Shola, and were very friendly and nice. It was part of a regular bit in *In Yer Face!* called *Chat 'n' Dance*. It went like this. Jez began, speaking to camera:

JEZ: Hey, we're so pleased to have with us the *biggest* child star since . . . what do you think, Shola?

SHOLA: The last one?

JEZ: Ha-ha!

SHOLA: D'you know what, Jez? I reckon he's bigger than that, to be honest! He's the biggest of the littlers!

JEZ: Well, exactly, Sholz. You know who we're talking about – give it up at home for the star of *School Daze*, Billy 'Relatabill' Smith!

At this point there was a lot of loud dance music, and Jez and Shola got up and did some moves. Then it stopped and they sat down again.

JEZ: How is it being famous, Billy?

BILLY: It's great! Don't you think so?

SHOLA: Ha-ha, we're not famous! We just

interview famous people.

JEZ: And dance in front of them!

The music started up again, and Jez and Shola danced some more. Then it stopped and they sat down again. This went on for some time, with them asking Billy loads more questions and doing loads more dancing. At the end – they always did this with the guests – he got up and danced too!

So Billy could have said any of these to Isla. But, as it happened, when an invitation *did* come from Isla Fawcett, for her birthday party, he just said 'yes, please', because by then he was quite happy to be invited to something normal for once.

CHAPTER 18
STYLISZTS

At all of these appearances, including, as explained, the fashion show, Billy just wore his ordinary clothes, a T-shirt and jeans. But for the film premiere, which was the biggest thing he'd been invited to so far, Stuart decided he needed to, in Stuart's words, 'up his threads'.

When Billy looked blank, Stuart said, 'Bring your sartorial A game.' When Billy continued to look blank, Stuart said, 'Oh my. Don't you understand

English? *Wear some smarter clothes!'*

But Billy didn't have a tuxedo or even a suit. He didn't have anything designed by anyone with an Italian name. Most of his clothes came from supermarkets.

Jane said, 'Don't worry, Billy, we'll buy you some nice new clothes from the internet.'

'Oh, from one of the designer websites?' said Billy.

'What? No, from a supermarket website.'

But then there was a knock on the door. They opened it. On the doorstep was Stuart, with two people, a man and a woman. They looked very similar: they were the same height, they both had black spiky hair, glasses, and both were wearing—

Well, let's see what Jane said.

'Hello,' said Billy's mum. 'Where did you get those outfits? We have people who wear those that work in our industrial freezer, shifting huge crates of fish.'

They stared at her.

'These, Jen,' said Stuart, 'are the latest in designer boiler suits. They are by Paninininini.'

'Pardon?'

'I may have said too many "nini"s. Anyway. Bill. Premiere of *Socks!* tomorrow, right?'

'Yes.'

Stuart flashed his very white teeth in a big smile. 'Billy, Jolene—'

'Jane,' said Jane.

'Right. Meet Sergio and Sergiana. Sergio is hair and make-up. Sergiana is clothes. Together, they are: Styliszts!'

There was a short pause. Sergio and Sergiana carried on staring at Billy.

'They are stylists?' said Billy.

'No.'

'No?'

'Well, yes, they are. But that isn't what I meant.

Their name is STYLISZTS!'

'Sergio Styliszts and Sergiana Styliszts?' said Jane.

'No!'

'Well, we are twins,' said Sergio, speaking for the first time, surprisingly in quite a strong northern British accent. 'So we *do* have the same surname.'

'Yes,' said Sergiana. 'Hickinbottom.'

'Well, don't tell them *that*!' said Stuart. 'Completely ruins the effect.'

CHAPTER 19
MONKEY SNOT

STYLISZTs – for that was indeed their team name – got to work. From a van outside, they carried into the house a tall chair and an even taller mirror, and set them up in the kitchen. Sergio had scissors and towels and a hair dryer and lots of jars of what he called 'product'. He lined these up very carefully on the windowsill.

Then he sat Billy in the chair, tied one of those black bibs round his neck and Billy shut his eyes.

Sergio held up the scissors. He took a very deep breath. Then another.

'Um . . . ?' said Billy. 'Are you—'

He was about to say 'OK?', but Sergio suddenly opened his eyes and swooped on him with the scissors.

Clip clip clip shape shape shape clip clip clip. Sometimes Sergio would stop and shut his eyes and do the deep-breath thing again, before diving back on to Billy's scalp. He seemed to be paying a *lot* of attention to it and taking a *lot* of time. This felt odd to Billy, who had always had the same haircut – short back and sides – his whole life. It had never occurred to him that you could do anything different with his hair.

'What kind of style are you thinking of?' asked Billy. He said this because he couldn't see what Sergio was doing. Unlike what normally happened when Billy had his hair cut (usually by a barber who took four minutes and charged £8), Sergio

wasn't letting him face the mirror. He had swung
the chair away from it.

'Shh!' said Sergiana. 'Never interrupt Sergio when he's creating.'

'Creating what?'

Sergiana stared at him. 'His *art*, of course.'

Billy wasn't sure about his hair being made into art, but it was too late. Suddenly, Sergio stopped clipping. He put the scissors down and surveyed his product range, intensely. He ran his fingers along the row, not actually touching any. He glanced at Sergiana.

'Deep Fix? Wet Stink? Extreme Hard Hold? Volume Up? Pump-it Pomade? Gummy Barnet? Candle Wax?'

'Candle Wax?' said Sergiana.

Sergio picked the pot up. 'Oh. This one actually is for candles.'

Sergiana came over. She held up one of the jars at the end of the row, which was brightly coloured and had a cartoon picture on it. Sergio took it from her and nodded.

'Monkey Snot! *Perfect!*'

'Um . . .' said Billy, but again it was too late. With a twist of Sergio's wrist, the jar was open, the fingers of his other hand were in, and Sergio had returned to Billy's head, rubbing it full of Monkey Snot. Finally, Sergio swung the chair back again to face the mirror. He undid the bib with a flourish and waved it across Billy's face to reveal, basically, a short back and sides. But spikier on top.

'Voilà!' said Sergio.

'Voilà indeed!' said Sergiana.

'You look like you're in a boy band, Billy,' said his mum.

'Yes,' said his dad, coming in. 'The one who's not going to have much of a solo career.'

Then it was Sergiana's turn.
She had brought with her a
selection of outfits, and she
asked Billy to try them all on. She
handed him each one on a hanger, and he went to his bedroom
and came back wearing them.
She called each outfit something.
This one she called **DISCO.**

This one was
Hell's Angel.

This one, **Scotsman.**

This one, **Fish-Man**.

And this one she called
A Boy Who Had Hoped
for More from Life.

Billy was wearing this outfit when Stuart came back to see how the makeover was going. Stuart looked at him. Billy wasn't sure if he was supposed to strike some kind of pose. He did his best, putting his hand on his hip, but that just made him look like a mad broken teapot.

Stuart frowned. 'Um . . . Sergiana. A word.'

'OK,' she said, raising an eyebrow.

'Billy's thing – Billy's brand – is normality. Ordinariness. *Relatabillyty*.'

'Do you mean . . . relatability?'

'No, I mean *relatabillyty*. It's a new word I've invented. And trademarked, actually. But it means the same thing.'

'Right.'

'But the point is . . .' he said, looking over to Billy, who was still trying to keep his mad broken teapot pose going, '*that* is a not a relatable outfit. That is an outfit that only someone who had fallen through a time tunnel, rolled about in some eighteenth-century pig muck and come back via Paris Fashion Week would wear. And, as far as I'm aware, that *isn't* most people.'

Sergio and Sergiana looked at each other. For a second, it looked like they might both storm out. But then Billy's mum, who had watched all this, said:

'He could just wear this . . .'

She had brought in his school uniform, from his bedroom. She held it out in front of her on a hanger.

'WHAT!' said Sergio and Sergiana together.

'Well . . .' said Jane, 'it's smart. And that's how most people know him. From the telly. And it's something loads of kids wear. So it's . . . um . . . "relatable".'

There was a silence. Sergio and Sergiana blinked at her, their eyes seeming to move in unison. Then everyone looked towards Stuart.

His hands moved up slowly into fists, and, for a second, Billy thought he might be about to explode in fury. But then, on top of his fists, both his thumbs went up, and his smile exploded instead.

'Sergiana! Get the uniform – and jazz it up a bit! Take that blazer, trousers and tie, and make them Prime Premiere Ready!' He turned on his heels towards the door, stopping only to say before leaving (still with his thumbs up):

'GREAT IDEA, JANE!'

Jane looked at Billy. 'He got my name right . . .' she said, in wonder.

CHAPTER 21
A DIFFERENT VOICE IN HIS HEAD

'**B**illy! Billy! Billy!'

Billy was, by now, used to other people saying his name excitedly. It happened all the time at school. But this was different. This was strangers. People who had only seen him on the telly! As he walked down the red carpet towards the cinema showing *Socks!*, there seemed to be *hundreds* of these people standing on either side of it, behind barriers. All calling:

'Billy!'   'Billy!'

'Billy!'

Some of them were waving autograph books and photos on cards and phones. And they were crying:

'Billy! Sign this!'

Or:

'Billy! Come and have a selfie with me!'

He was walking down the red carpet with Bo and Rinor. He got to take two friends with him, and had asked Bo because she, like him, was a big Pixar fan. In fact, they'd once spent three hours talking about whether *Ratatouille* or *Toy Story 3* was the better film, before they finally decided that it was *Coco*. But they still thought that the scene where Antoine Ego tastes the first mouthful of Remy's ratatouille was the greatest moment in cinema. Bo was wearing a red-and-white tracksuit and trainers. This might have been because she didn't know she was meant to dress up for a premiere. Or because she didn't care. Or, most likely, because Bo knew she still looked cool in a red-and-white tracksuit and trainers.

Billy had also asked Rinor because he too was a big film fan, but also because Billy was intrigued as to what his friend might wear. Sure enough, Rinor, on his parents' insistence, was wearing the traditional green hunting suit of the vicinity of Balmadömölk, which consisted of long, flappy shorts and a large, pointy hat made out of goatskin.

Billy had come, as suggested, in his school uniform, only it had been, using Sergio's word, 'accessorised'. Translated, this meant that some shiny metallic bits and pieces had been stuck on the blazer.

'This is amazing, Billy!' Bo said. 'Everyone knows who you are!'

'Yes!' he said. And then a strange thought appeared in his mind, unexpectedly: *Well, of course they do. Of course they do, Bo. I'm the star of* School Daze. But it felt weird, almost like someone else – someone who wasn't him – had come into his head and said it.

'Look, they're all reaching out towards you! Are you going to sign stuff for them?' Bo continued. Billy really wanted to, but he wasn't sure he was allowed. He turned round. Walking behind him were his parents. His dad was wearing a tuxedo, which is that black suit that people wear with a bow tie at glamorous events. 'I feel like a waiter,' he'd said when Sergiana helped him into it (because Styliszts also dressed Jane and John for the event).

'Waiters haven't dressed like this since 1972,' Sergiana had replied. 'Most restaurants now, the waiters look like tramps with designer glasses.'

Meanwhile, Billy's mum was in a sparkly blue dress that was actually hers. It was the poshest thing she owned, and she'd never had an opportunity to wear it out before. 'Mum,' Billy had said, before they left. 'I've never seen you look like that before. You look beautiful.' And she'd started crying, which meant that Sergio had got furious, shouting: 'Now we'll have to do all your make-up again!'

The baby, in case you're worried, was at home with a babysitter. Who had got Billy to sign an autograph for her.

'Hey, Bill!' said his dad, looking at the crowd. 'They all know who you are!'

'Yes,' said Billy, suppressing once again the thought *Of course they do!* 'Is it OK if I go and sign some things?'

His mum and dad looked a bit uncertain. But then Stuart appeared, also wearing a tuxedo. A much more expensive-looking one than John's. He did his double thumbs up, and his smile.

'*Can* you? Ha! What do you think you're here for?' he said.

'To see the film, mainly,' said Bo.

'Oh. Hello, Bo. Yes, I'm not sure what *you're* here for.'

'Pardon, Stuart?'

'I'm going over!' said Billy, running over to one side of the carpet, where all the people were.

The first person he went up to – a teenage girl who was shouting, 'Billy! Over here! Do mine first!' – was waving a photo at him. It was him! It was the one that had been in the paper, above the review of *School Daze* – him reading out his essay – but she had blown it up to about three times its original size and mounted it on a piece of card. 'Sign here, please! Maybe on the back of your essay!' she said, handing him a pen (which meant that Billy didn't have to take out the pen he'd got handy for giving autographs).

And Billy signed. He signed his new signature – the one he'd practised for ages. After he'd done it, he looked at it. It looked good. It looked right. It looked like a proper signature. He handed the photo back to her, and she held it up, shouting, 'Look! I got Billy! Billy Smith!' Then other people crowded around, asking for more signatures. People also wanted to have selfies with him, putting their arms round him and pulling him towards them while grinning madly into their phones. Billy tried to do them all,

but there were too many hands, too many photos, too many phones, and, eventually, Bo shouted:

'Oi! Are we going to see this movie or what?'

Billy looked over. She was standing on the red carpet with her arms folded, tapping her foot. Rinor had taken off his goatskin hat. It looked like he was sweating quite a lot.

Another thought came into Billy's head. *Oh, yes: I'd forgotten about the film.* But, again, with that strange feeling that it wasn't quite him thinking it. Like it was a different voice in his head.

'Coming!' he said, and, saying sorry to some of the people who were still trying to get him to sign things, he extricated himself from the crowd. He noticed some of them looked quite upset that he had never got round to them.

Billy also noticed that, after he'd gone, they just started shouting the names of other celebrities walking down the red carpet. But that didn't matter. That meant he was one of them. *A celebrity.*

CHAPTER 22
SUNSHINE DE MARTO

'OMG, Billy. That was so great. I loved it when Pink, the hero sock, decided that she loved Blue sock more than Also-Pink sock, even though the laws of Sock Drawer City say you have to match up to your own colour; and then I loved it more when she got lost in Tumble Dryer Town amongst all the other laundry and had to find her way back with her new for-some-reason-British friends, Sir Pants and Lady Vest, who taught her so much about just being who you are and living your own life, so that by the time she actually made it back to Sock Drawer City she got rolled into a loving ball with Blue and then ended up on the feet of the man who owned them, because it turned out he didn't care about not wearing matching socks in the first place!'

Breathlessly going over the entire plot of a movie was something Bo did a lot, especially with Pixar films. Billy nodded along as she spoke – he had enjoyed the film a lot too – but he wasn't quite listening. They were at the post-premiere party, and Billy was looking over at the middle of the huge room they were standing in, where a circle of people were cut off from the rest of the party by a purple velvet rope. The party was very exciting. There was music and dancing and flashing lights and free food – cupcakes in the shape of socks, Lady Vest sandwiches, and a slightly misjudged Sir Pants chocolate cake – and loads of people milling around saying, 'Hi! How great to see you!' and 'Call me!' But Billy could see that the biggest celebrities had all been ushered into the little circle inside that velvet rope.

'You know,' said Rinor, 'Barry Bennett says he went to a film premiere. When he was in that world run by children . . .'

'Oh, yes,' said Bo. 'He saw a film called *Death in the Car V.*'

'Yes,' said Billy, feeling a bit irritated suddenly. 'But no one believes *that* really happened. All the famous people just had silly made-up names. Like Monty and the Nose Hairs and Dickie Henderson-Bear. Meanwhile, look who's here!' He pointed to the velvet-roped circle.

Bo and Rinor looked over. Bo squinted. 'Um . . . is that the man who does that advert with the talking toy dog?' she said.

'Oh, yes,' said Rinor. 'And look – there's that

lady who sings a song about carpet cleaner while cleaning a carpet.'

'Are you sure? I think it's the person who came third in *I'm Famous, Don't Put Me in a Box with Insects!* two years ago,' said Bo.

'Hmm. That might be the same woman.'

'Look,' said Billy, finding himself getting more irritated, 'this place is *full* of famous people!' He looked over. 'I mean, there's . . . there's . . . and there's . . .'

The trouble was, a lot of the people behind the velvet rope, although they all looked familiar – and, certainly, they were all carrying themselves as if they were very famous indeed, smiling and talking loudly and generally giving off loads of confidence – were not actually people who he could place by name. But then a loud voice said:

'OK, make way! Come on! Get out of the way!'

Billy looked round. It was Stuart. He was making

his way across the room towards the velvet-roped circle. Behind him were two men and two women in suits and dark glasses. They all had head mics, and were all looking around suspiciously at everyone else there. Together, they formed a human rectangle, moving slowly forwards.

And in the middle of that rectangle was Sunshine De Marto.

CHAPTER 23
THE MUGGLES BIT

It was the first time Billy had seen Sunshine De Marto in real life. It was not a disappointment. Although she was looking down, Billy could tell she looked *amazing*. She'd dyed her hair a new colour, of course – a brilliant shade of orange. She was carrying, under each arm, Mindy and Mandy, her two tiny Chiwaapoos. She just radiated, in his mind, star power. She didn't have to even look up for everyone at the party to stare at her.

Although, that was probably also partly caused by Stuart continuing to shout, loudly:

'Let's go! Open the rope! Sunshine coming through! Billys stand back!'

They got to the velvet rope. Immediately, a woman in a blue suit and glasses, who had been standing there with a clipboard, unhooked a bit of the rope that formed a gate into the circle. She stepped back, allowing Sunshine and the people around her to go in. Then she clipped the rope back again.

'OMG, there's Sunshine De Marto!' said Bo, unnecessarily.

'I can't believe it!' said Rinor. 'It's really her!'

'Let's go over there!'

Bo looked at Billy. 'Are we allowed?'

Billy felt nervous, unsure what to do. But he nodded.

'Yes. I'm sure.'

When they got to the velvet rope, the blue-suited lady was still standing there. She didn't even look up from her clipboard.

'What?' she said.

Bo and Rinor looked at Billy.

'Um . . . can we come in? To this bit?' said Billy.

'I don't think so,' she said, chuckling. She managed to chuckle *throughout* saying it, as if every single word had a laugh underneath it.

Billy frowned. He didn't know what to say. His two friends were looking at him. Then the new voice – the one that didn't feel quite like his own – came into his head, suggesting something he *could* say. Even with everything that had happened to him, it felt stupid. But then he found the words coming out of his mouth anyway.

'Look, don't you know who I am . . . ?'

The woman in the blue suit looked up. She took off her glasses, and frowned. She shook her head. She raised an eyebrow. She adopted a sneery expression and was definitely about to say 'No' when a voice said:

'Of course she does!'

It was Stuart, who had appeared next to the woman. The woman's whole attitude completely changed. She looked suddenly nervous.

'Um . . . I do?'

'You do!' said Stuart. 'This, Lulu my dear, is – obviously – one of TV's biggest stars presently. It's . . . ?'

The blue-suited woman – Lulu – stared at Billy. She was clearly starting to panic.

'Yes. Obviously. I knew. I was just joking.' She unhooked the velvet rope. 'Welcome to the VIP area . . . um . . .'

There was a long pause.

'Billy. Billy Smith,' said Billy.

'I WAS JUST GOING TO SAY THAT! WELL! YOU LIKE TO GET IN FAST, DON'T YOU, BILLY SMITH?' she said, loudly, and mainly towards Stuart.

'From *School Daze.*'

'FROM *SCHOOL DAYS*! OF COURSE!'

'With a Z.'

'*SCHOOL DAYS* WITH A Z! WHAT A SHOW THAT IS!'

Visibly sweating, Lulu stepped aside, to allow Billy into the VIP area. Billy walked in. Then Lulu clipped the rope back shut again. Behind Billy. Billy turned round.

'What about my friends?'

'Sorry?' said Lulu.

'You haven't let my friends in . . .'

Bo and Rinor were, indeed, still on the other side of the velvet rope.

'Oh . . .' Lulu looked down at her clipboard. Then she looked at Stuart, who had been watching all this. 'Um . . . ?'

'Yes. Here's the thing, Billy,' said Stuart. 'The VIP area –' he pronounced it as one word, 'vip' – 'is a special place just for . . . you know . . . *stars*. Not Billys.'

'But I'm a Billy.'

'Yes, but you're not an ordinary.'

'But I thought you said I *was* ordinary.'

Stuart glanced at Bo and Rinor.

'Some people are more ordinary than others,' he said. 'Anyway, it's complicated. Best not to think too hard about it. Either way, it's a bit crowded in here just at the minute. So, really, I think maybe say ta-ta to Bob and Tina for now. You can always meet up later back in the Billys . . .' He looked at Billy, who was still clearly confused, '. . . in the Muggles bit.'

Billy looked up at Stuart. 'Um . . .' he said. He felt he should argue. That he should insist that his friends *had* to be allowed into the VIP area. That they were coming in, or *he* wasn't coming in. But he didn't feel quite brave enough, and also he really *did* want to be in there, because Sunshine De Marto was – and, while he was thinking about all that, Stuart had disappeared.

Billy looked round, towards his friends, outside the velvet rope. 'Did you hear that?' he said.

But Bo and Rinor were already walking away.

CHAPTER 24
★ A SWISH OF ORANGE HAIR ★

Seconds later, Billy was zipping around the VIP area, looking for Sunshine. He couldn't see her anywhere.

'Hi, aren't you that kid from that school doc?' a bald man said to him. 'Billy, right?'

'Yes,' Billy said. The bald man looked at him, like he was expecting Billy to say something else. Eventually, he sighed and said:

'I'm Derek. The man from the Reassure Insurance

advert. You know the one with the talking toy dog?'

'Oh, right!' said Billy. 'Pleased to meet you.'

'This is my friend Linda. She sings that song about carpets in that carpet-cleaning one.'

'Well,' said the middle-aged woman next to Derek – clearly Linda – 'I also won *I'm Famous, Don't Put Me in a Box with Insects!* two years ago.'

'I thought you came third?' said Derek.

'OK, don't go on about it, Derek.'

'Excuse me,' said Billy, 'have either of you seen Sunshine De Marto? I know she just came in here.'

Derek looked up, and pointed. Billy followed the direction of his finger.

'There she is,' said Derek.

Walking away from the VIP area, indeed walking out of the building, was the human rectangle surrounding Sunshine De Marto. Billy caught just a swish of her orange hair as she exited the door.

'Yeah. She never stays anywhere very long,

does she, Derek?' said Linda.

'No,' said Derek. 'Anyway, Billy, let me tell you more about insurance . . .'

CHAPTER 25

THE MONTAGE SEQUENCE 2: RETURN OF THE MONTAGE SEQUENCE

It was at this point, looking at Sunshine's orange hair disappearing from the party, surrounded by her entourage, that Billy realised something.

What had just happened – nearly bumping into Sunshine De Marto – had happened before.

In fact, maybe it had happened before more than once, now he thought about it.

For example, at the fashion show, as he'd swerved round to roller skate back up the runway, he'd seen a flash of purple hair in the audience, and thought, *Oh . . . that looks like Sunshine's hair! Is that her?* So he'd swerved again to look back in case it was. And fallen over. This got a very big laugh from the audience.

Then he'd fallen over again when he tried to get up and couldn't because his wheeled feet were flying out backwards beneath him. Luckily, afterwards, everyone decided that him falling over was very 'on brand' and Relatabill. However, it did mean that by the time he got backstage and changed out of the skates to go and look for her the young woman with the purple hair – if it was Sunshine – was gone.

At Burger Munch, just as he was about to tuck into his food, he'd looked out of the window and noticed a human rectangle in suits, surrounding a beautiful girl with deep-green hair going into Pie. Could it be her again? He was about to say: 'Hey, everyone, let's go back and eat in Pie after all!' but by then he could see his dad was already halfway through his Super-Size Deep-Fried Big Fishy.

Then there was the time at the spiritual guru's house, at the end of the session, when Astral had woken them all up (it had taken a while with John, who'd started saying, 'Where's my cup of tea, Mum?' before realising where he was). They'd picked up the baby, and got in their car, which was parked in Astral's front drive. Astral had come out, still wearing the blanket, but now underneath quite a big anorak. He'd put his palms together, and said:

'Peace. Goodbye.'

Billy had put his hands together as well, although his mum just waved. His dad continued to look sleepy as he strapped Lisa into her car seat, got into his own seat, started the car and pressed the window button for it to go up.

'Sorry,' said his dad, yawning, 'Haven't had such a good kip in ages.'

'Yes, all right,' said Astral. 'Can you go now? I've got someone rather important coming in five minutes. Ah, here she is!'

At which point, Billy saw a large black car driving up the road towards the house. In the back, he thought he saw a sliver of bobbing pink colour, exactly the kind of hair that he associated with Sunshine. He wanted to ask Astral if it was her, but the window shut and, before he knew it, his dad had driven off.

And then at *In Yer Face!*, on his way out of the studio, he had said, 'Thank you very much. Who have you got on tomorrow?'

'Oh!' said Jez. 'Tomorrow's a big one.'

'Not that you weren't!' said Shola.

'Hey! No. Don't get me wrong. You're so hot right now.'

'I feel OK,' said Billy. 'Although maybe I should take my jumper off?'

'No . . .' said Jez. 'It means, like, hot. With the kids. And the press. Everyone's interested in you!'

'Oh. Thanks!'

'But tomorrow,' said Shola, 'we've got an exclusive. With Sun—'

'Hey!' said Jez. 'Zip it. Not allowed. Embargoed.'

Billy stopped. 'I won't tell anyone . . .'

Jez laughed. 'Well, let's not say her – I'm prepared to say it's a *her* – name, then.'

Billy nodded. He said, a little uncertainly, 'So does . . . *she* watch this show?'

'She's a fan!' said Shola. 'So she was keen to come on.'

Billy thought about this.

'So . . . do you think she'll be watching this one . . . ?' he said.

'Yeah! Never misses an episode,' said Jez.

Billy nodded. He was pleased because this meant that he was in some sort of contact with Sunshine. Or, at least, he was if they were actually talking about *her*. But he still felt a bit confused as to why it was that, although she never missed an episode of *In Yer Face!*, he always seemed to be missing her wherever he went.

Just like now, again, at the premiere of *Socks!*

Billy stood for a while, in the VIP area, staring at the space where Sunshine had been. Even though he was now famous, it seemed he was never actually going to meet Sunshine De Marto.

CHAPTER 26
THE FAIRLY RUBBISH CLIMBING FRAME

Billy felt bad about what had happened to Bo and Rinor at the premiere. He decided that he should apologise for it the next day at school. He was in the playground, and was just about to go over to where they were standing, by the fairly rubbish climbing frame, when a hand was placed on his shoulder.

'Hello, Billy!'

Billy looked round. A woman who didn't look that much older than himself, but who was still definitely a grown-up, was looking down at him. She was wearing some kind of pink hat, which Billy thought might have been a beret, but given he wasn't entirely sure what a beret was he couldn't say definitely. In her other hand she held an enormous phone.

'Um . . . hello?'

'I'm Suz. I'm your new publicist.'

'You are?'

'Yep. I work with **TOTALPR** PR. I thought I'd just come down before school starts and intro myself.'

'OK . . .' Billy nodded. 'I don't really know what a publicist does.'

'Oh, you know – brand control, reputation management, basic PR, online admin, digital influencing, marketing pitches, et cetera, et cetera . . .'

'Right,' said Billy, not having understood a word she'd said. 'Well, I just need to go and apologise to my friends.'

Her hand tightened on his shoulder.

'Uh . . . an apology?' Suz had lowered her voice, but increased its intensity. Like people do when they've heard something really dramatic.

'Um. Yes.'

She looked around. Then crouched down so that she was nearer his face.

'OK, I think we need to think about this before you do anything. If you're going to apologise for something, publicly, maybe we should word it very carefully first? Don't want to end up causing *more* offence. Or maybe: have you thought about doing it on camera? And then putting it out on social media?'

Billy shook his head.

'Either way, we should wargame it. Write a script. *Crisis manage.* Maybe we could schedule it in for next week and put together a comms timeline? Is it possible you might cry during the apology? That always plays well with a certain demographic.'

Billy shook his head again, although a part of him did feel a bit like crying: the part that was totally confused by what this woman was saying.

'Is it possible, Billy?' said another voice. He looked round. It was Bo, who'd come over, and had clearly been listening for a while.

'Um . . . I don't think so. I just wanted to say sorry. That you and Rinor didn't get into the VIP area at the premiere. I felt bad about it . . . I'll do my best to make sure nothing like that happens again.'

Bo nodded. 'That's OK.' She looked around. 'Do you want to come and swing from the fairly rubbish climbing frame?'

'Sure,' said Billy. And they ran over to the fairly rubbish climbing frame together.

Suz watched them go, shook her head and made a note in her extremely large phone: *Work on Billy's apologising skills*.

CHAPTER 27
PRINZE NOIZE

'**M**y name is Billy and . . . my name is . . . um . . .'

The music stopped with a thud. The producer looked at Billy through the glass window he was sitting behind.

'Sorry, I forgot the words.' Billy felt he should say something else, to make it not completely his fault. So he said: 'I can't hear the bass that well?'

'No worries, Billy. I'll turn the bass up on the sample. And let's go again. One more time!'

Once again, Billy's famousness had placed him somewhere he had never thought he would ever find himself: in a recording studio. The person speaking to him, through his headphones, was called Prinze Noize, and he was a famous rap producer (although his real name was Ivor). Billy was sitting on a stool, in front of a large microphone. Prinze Noize was behind a massive recording desk in the other room. Billy could see him through a big sheet of glass. Behind him was Stuart, who did his usual smile and a big thumbs up at Billy. He leant over and spoke into a microphone.

'And remember, Billy – we want to hear *your* voice now. Someone else did it on the internet, but we've closed that down, legally, and so now it's time for you to do the official version. This is about Billy Smith making the Relatabill Rap his own!'

'Why didn't he write the lyrics, then?' said Prinze Noize, under his breath.

'Not helpful, Mr Noize,' said Stuart.

Billy heard the start of the track come through on his headphones. The bass *was* much louder. *BOOM BOOM BA-BOOM BOOM BUP!* it went in his ears. He looked up. Prinze Noize raised a finger in his direction, meaning *Now!*

Billy began:

'My name is Billy

I'm not so silly

In fact, truth is——'

'I've got a ten-foot willy!'

'OK. Who said that?' said Stuart, as the music stopped again.

There was a short silence. Then there was a burst of giggling from Billy. Then Bo, who had been sitting in the corner of the studio, put her hand up.

'I see,' said Stuart. 'Right. I'm calling a meeting of Hashtag Team Billy! Everyone in the coffee room. Now!'

Bo got up. Billy got off his stool.

'Why does Stuart always call it "Hashtag Team Billy"?' said Billy. 'He's speaking in real life, not on social media?'

'I'm not sure Stuart is ever speaking in real life,' said Bo, darkly.

CHAPTER 28
A MEETING OF HASHTAG TEAM BILLY

'**R**ight!' said Stuart, when they had all gathered together in the coffee room. 'Hashtag Team Billy!'

Bo put her hand up.

'Don't ask him about the hashtag,' whispered Billy.

Bo put her hand down. In the room, as well as her and Billy and Stuart, were Dan, Natasha, Styliszts Sergio and Sergiana, Suz the publicist (now wearing an orange beret) and Billy's parents. Lisa was asleep in a sling that Jane was wearing.

Jane put her hand up.

'Janelle, yep?' said Stuart.

'Inside voice, please, Stuart,' said Jane, indicating the baby.

'OK, yeah,' said Stuart, hardly changing the volume of his voice at all. 'So. Things are going great. In general. I would say. Wouldn't you, Suz?'

Suz glanced at her phone, which seemed to have, in a month, grown bigger than ever. She had to hold it with two hands.

'Yuh, right – sure – I just checked Billy's pages. Insta: 700K followers. The Tok: 500K. YouTube subscribers: 60K. The old persons' ones – Twitter, Facebook – all pretty high too. I don't check them so much. Oh, and we've got *loads*, like cray-cray loads, of requests for interviews and stuff from "newspapers", whatever they are. I'll get on to them at some point.'

'Right,' said Stuart. 'So that all sounds very good.

But *something* is still slowing us down. Something is still holding up Billy getting from the top – I mean, don't get me wrong, the *very* top – of the B list, to the *very* top of the A plus plus plus list!'

'Maybe we need someone,' said Dan, 'to help him along. You know . . . someone with a bit of A-plus-plus-plus-list star power themselves? To just come and hang out and maybe do some filming and some photos with Billy. Sort of a statement, like, "We, the *really* famous, think of him as one of us."'

'Good idea, Dan. A photo op. Great. But who?' Stuart turned to the group. 'Hit me with your ideas, guys.'

'Six Bananas?' said Prinze Noize. No one said anything.

'Fast Charge?' said Suz. Still nothing. And then:

'Sunshine De Marto?' said a voice.

It wasn't, in fact, Billy's. It was Bo's.

'Hey, yeah!' said Dan 'Of course!'

'Right!' said Natasha.

'Billy does *really* like her,' said Jane Smith.

'Who is she again?' said John.

'Oh, John! I've told you millions of times!'

'Yuh, her influhitz isn't quite as big as it was,' said Suz. 'But—'

'Sorry, her what?' said Dan.

'Influhitz. How many hits she gets as an influencer.'

'Oh.'

'But, sure – she's still dope. She's still the GOAT. Gucci. Lit. Optimal.'

'On fleek . . . ?' said Stuart, uncertainly.

'No one says that any more,' said Suz, looking pained.

'Yes, well, obviously,' said Stuart. 'Anyway. Sunshine would be great . . . amazing, but . . .'

Billy frowned. He'd realised something, which was that, ever since all this started, he'd been feeling very *grateful* to Stuart. And everyone else from **TOTALTV** TV and **TOTALPR** PR. And when Stuart said 'but . . .' a thought suddenly occurred to him. It, again, came to him in that strange tone that didn't feel like it was quite his own voice. It was a more confident voice than his usual one, but also colder, more superior. He noticed that this tone was becoming more and more familiar to him, and these thoughts were feeling more and more like his own. The thought was: *Hang on. I don't work for these people. THEY work for ME.*

'But *what*, Stuart?' he said, loudly.

Stuart looked at him, surprised. Billy didn't normally sound quite so definite when speaking to him.

'Well, Billy . . . she's very busy—'

'I know,' said Billy, continuing in his new tone. 'Very busy indeed, it seems. But I seem to remember that when I agreed to be represented by **TOTALTV** TV, you said that it'd be no bother at all if I wanted to meet Sunshine. In fact, I'm sure of it. That's what you said.'

'I did. You're absolutely right.'

'So how come every time I *nearly* meet her, I don't?'

'Yes,' said Bo, evidently feeling the need to stick up for Billy. 'Why not?'

Stuart narrowed his eyes at Bo. Then something seemed to occur to him. An idea. 'OK. Here's the deal,' he said. 'I agree that Sunshine De Marto is the perfect celebrity to . . . *position* with Billy at this moment. I also accept that as a company we did promise to put them together at some point and have failed to do so. So. This is what I suggest. You know your PA, Billy?'

'This one?' said Billy, pointing to his dad.

'No. Not your *pa*. Your PA. Personal appearance. The big one you've got coming up. At Clubability.'

'Oh, yes!' said Billy. He'd been asked to do so much since he got famous that he'd started to forget a lot of where he was meant to be. A personal appearance was something that famous people did, where they just turned up somewhere, and waved and said hello and signed autographs and chatted to the audience that came to see them. He hadn't done one yet, but **TOTALPR** PR had booked Clubability, one of the hottest nightclubs of the moment, for Billy to do his first PA next week.

'It's going to be great,' said Dan. 'A thousand people are coming!'

'Wow! Really?' said Billy.

'Yep,' said Stuart. 'I will have a word with Sunshine's people—'

'I thought you *were* Sunshine's people.'

Stuart considered this. 'We are. Yes. You're right. So that makes it much easier. And we'll make sure she's there. But, here's the thing, Billy: Sunshine De Marto – she doesn't just *turn up* to events. Things have to be just right. We *must* make sure that everything is just so. You know – the mood; the temperature; the team.'

'Right . . .' said Billy. 'So . . . ?'

'So I think if Sunshine is going to come into –' his fingers did a swirling motion – 'this environment, we need to make sure she only meets *positive* people. People who are on the same page. Page "Hashtag Team Billy" *stroke* "Hashtag Team Sunshine". And to do that I think we might need to slim Hashtag Team Billy down a bit.'

'Right,' said Billy, again. 'So . . . ?'

'Oh, for goodness' sake, Billy,' said Bo, standing up. 'He means me.'

'He does?'

'Have you not noticed he's been looking at me the whole time he's been talking?'

'Um . . . I thought that was maybe because his head had got stuck.'

'No, his head hasn't got stuck. He's been staring

right at me deliberately while he's been talking about the need to slim down Hashtag Team Billy. I *know* Stuart means me. Even though I still don't know why he has to say "Hashtag".'

Billy looked up at Stuart. Stuart shrugged, in a way that clearly meant: *Well, yeah, I meant Bo.*

'Oh,' said Billy.

'Yes,' said Bo. 'So,' she said, 'what do *you* think, Billy? Do you think Hashtag Team Billy needs to slim down by one Bo?'

CHAPTER 29
HIS NEW VOICE

'**U**m . . .' said Billy. He didn't know what to do. He felt pulled in different directions at once. He *really* wanted to be nice to his friend, and to keep his promise not to exclude her from things he got invited to any more . . . but he also did *really really* want to meet Sunshine De Marto. And it seemed as if Stuart was saying if Sunshine was coming, then Bo had to go.

Billy was not a complicated boy. In his life,

until he had become famous, he hadn't had to deal much with complicated feelings, with being pulled in different directions at once. But it did seem like fame brought a *lot* of that sort of thing with it.

Stuart, meanwhile, had got his phone out. He turned it towards Billy. There was a photo on it. A photo of Sunshine De Marto. With silver hair. Smiling. Looking very beautiful, but also very friendly. And it wasn't just a photo. It was a photo that was attached to Sunshine's name in Stuart's contacts. He waved the phone in front of Billy, and raised an eyebrow.

'Shall I call her now?' he said. Evilly. I'd like to use another adverb here, but there isn't really a better one.

Billy turned round, and saw that Bo had started walking towards the door. Billy felt suddenly angry. Partly because he didn't know how to feel about this, but also angry with Bo, because it felt like it *was* sort of her fault. He shouted after her:

'OK, Bo! Walk out! It never feels like you want to be here anyway! Or, actually, it's like you want to be

here, but you're cross about how you got here! Like you want to come to all the exciting things that you get invited to now because of me being famous, but when you get there you're just envious and angry with me for being the famous one!'

Bo, who had reached the studio door by the time Billy had finished shouting this, stopped for a second. In that moment, Billy realised that all those words that had just come out of his mouth had been spoken entirely in his new voice that wasn't quite his own, the one that was colder and more superior to his normal one.

He felt an urge to say, *Sorry, Bo, I don't know why I'm speaking in this voice. Or why I said all those things. Really I don't.*

But before he actually did say that, without turning round, Bo opened the door and left.

CHAPTER 30
MACARONI CHEESE ON THE TELLY

'**S**o . . . Billy,' said Billy's mum. 'Are you looking forward to your personal appearance at Clubability? Are a lot of people coming?'

'Cut!' said Stuart.

'I have already,' said Natasha.

They were filming a new episode of *At Home with the Ordinarys*. Billy, his mum, his dad and the baby were all in the living room, pretending there wasn't a camera crew in there with them. The TV news was on.

'Sorry, was that wrong?' said Jane.

'Janey . . .' said Stuart, coming out from behind the camera.

'She never calls herself that,' said John.

'Shh, John,' said Jane. 'It's closer than he normally gets.'

'The last thing we do on *At Home with the Ordinarys* is talk shop.'

'Talk shop? Which shop? I never mentioned a shop.'

'Shop, dear. The business. The one we used to call show.'

At that point, the baby started crying. Jane picked her up. 'There, there, Lisa. I have no idea what he's saying either.'

'Filming again,' said Natasha. 'I got some good shots of the baby.'

Stuart nodded, but he didn't seem to be listening to her.

'Mum,' said Billy, 'what he means is – don't talk about my famousness.'

'Oh! Right.' She frowned. 'Why not?'

'Yes,' said John. 'Seems a bit odd. As your famousness is definitely the most exciting thing around here!'

'Yes, but that's not what the Billys want from this show,' said Stuart.

'There's only one of him,' said John, pointing. 'He's over there.'

'That's what he calls— Oh, never mind,' said Billy.

'But the problem is, Stuart . . . that *is* what we talk about. At the moment,' said Jane.

Then, as if to make her point, the news ended, and a trailer popped up on the TV: '*Later tonight, it's another episode of everyone's favourite documentary,* School Daze!' said the voice-over. Suddenly, there was a shot of Bracket Wood, and there was Billy, not just on the sofa watching TV, but on the TV looking out at them on the sofa!

'*What's Relatabill Billy Smith been up to this week?*' the voice-over continued.

'*I'm hoping to be early enough in the queue for lunch to get macaroni cheese this week,*' said Billy on the TV.

'See!' said Stuart. 'That's the kind of thing people want from Billy! Ordinariness!'

'But it's not ordinary!' said Jane.

'Macaroni cheese isn't ordinary?' said Stuart. He sounded genuinely confused, as if he'd never eaten any (which possibly he hadn't).

'Not *macaroni cheese*! Watching your son talk about macaroni cheese *on the telly!*'

'*Billy Smith: what a star!*' said the voice-over.

Billy's mum and dad stared at Stuart. Billy carried on looking at the TV. *What a star*, he mouthed, perhaps without realising he was doing it.

'Shall I cut again?' said Natasha.

CHAPTER 31
★ THAT'S MY BRAND ★

'So . . . what do I actually do?' said Billy.

'Pardon?' said Jez.

'When the audience are here. To see me. Tonight. What do I do?'

'Um . . .' Jez frowned.

It was a week later. They were sitting onstage at Clubability. The stage looked out on to a very big, presently empty, dance floor. Jez and Shola, who were going to be hosting the event, were sitting on high stools. Billy was sitting facing them on an equally high stool. Slightly too high, if truth be known. He looked like he might topple off at any moment.

'Not sure anyone's asked that about a PA before,' said Shola.

'Well, you stand offstage,' said Jez. 'We get the audience going—'

'We say things like –' Shola turned to the empty room, and raised her voice, like the crowd were already there – 'You lucky, lucky people! Have we got a treat for you tonight!'

Jez also looked out over the room and raised his voice:

'It's the big one tonight! The hottest of the hot! In years to come, you'll be telling your children that you were there, the night Clubability had a personal appearance from . . .'

'You know who!' said Shola. 'He's waiting for us now in the wings! Give it up, wave your hands in the air, shout and scream and generally go wild for . . .'

She turned and lowered her voice. 'And then we say your name. And you come on.'

'Yes, but then what do I *do*?' said Billy.

Jez and Shola exchanged glances. 'You wave at them. You say, "Hello, everyone!" We have a little chat . . . and then you go off.'

Billy stared at them. 'That's it?'

'Um . . . yes,' said Shola.

'One thousand people are coming to see me do *that*?'

'Um . . . yes,' said Jez.

'Wow . . .' said Billy, looking out, and imagining the audience all there, all excited to see him. 'I guess I really am a big star.'

Jez and Shola nodded, a little awkwardly. Jez said:

'Um . . . one of the things about being famous, Billy, is . . .'

'Yes?'

'Well, you're not really supposed to *say* that you're famous.'

Billy frowned. 'You're not?'

'No,' said Shola. 'You're supposed to be . . . you know . . . humble, and stuff.'

'Oh, yes. And *ordinary*. Of course. That's my brand!' He laughed. 'Sorry, I forgot.' Billy looked out into the hall, where Stuart and Suz were watching. 'Don't worry, Stu! I won't say anything like that tonight. Out loud. I'll be very much playing the *ordinary* card. My ordinariness will be set to full blast!'

He winked at Jez and Shola. They didn't wink back. They just looked a bit embarrassed.

'OK . . .' said Shola. 'Anyway, obviously, also, halfway through that bit, we'll bring on Sunshine. People don't know she's coming so that'll be amazing for the audience.'

'Great!' said Billy, starting to get off his stool. 'So exciting!' Then he stopped. 'Hold on. Sorry. Just checking what you said there – she's a surprise?'

'Yes,' said Jez.

'The audience don't know about Sunshine? And still a thousand people are coming tonight?'

'Yes,' said Shola.

'Goodness me,' said Billy. 'I am *such* a big star.' They looked at him, open-mouthed. He chuckled and did a thumbs up. 'Don't worry, I won't be saying that tonight.' He shifted on his seat, looked down to the ground and then held the same thumb out to Jez. 'By the way, can you help me down from this stool?'

CHAPTER 32
★ WHISPERING PEACH ★

Later that night, Billy was waiting in his dressing room, which was a little way from the stage. It was a large room, with windows, but the curtains (all white) were shut – 'to stop the Billys peeking in,' Stuart had said when he'd come by earlier. There were a lot of mirrors in there, surrounded by shining light bulbs. There was a big basket of fruit. There was a coffee pot, and some cups, even though Billy didn't drink coffee. And there was a row of clothes on a rack of hangers against the wall. All of these were his school uniform: trousers, blazers, shirts and tie. Ten different versions of it. All exactly the same.

Next to his was another one. That was where Sunshine De Marto was going to be. He could hear Styliszts in there, making it ready.

'OK, Sergiana,' said Sergio. 'Here are the freshly cut roses. Where should they go?'

'Well, we've already got twenty-seven bouquets—'

'That's what she has to have. Twenty-eight bouquets – a dozen roses in each, all fresh.'

'Yes, I've put them all in new white vases.'

'The vases have to be exactly one and a half feet apart.'

'I know that, Sergio. I haven't been looking after Sunshine for five months without knowing that!'

'OK. Have you done the temperature control?'

'Yes, exactly twenty point seven degrees.'

'Nibbles?'

'Doggy-caviar drops at the ready.'

'Good. And for her?'

'Fifteen small plates of M&Ms. Only green ones.'

'Background ambient sounds?'

'Whale-song and tropical waterfall MP3s at the ready.'

'Mineral water?'

'Eternal Spring, gently carbonated. Twelve bottles.'

'Candles?'

'Yes. This Smells Like My Back Garden, by Sloop. I've got a hundred of those ready to be lit—'

'Wait a minute . . . talking of smells . . .' Sergio sniffed the air. 'That isn't fresh paint.'

There was a silence. 'Yes, it is.'

'From when?'

'Yesterday.'

'Yesterday? Yesterday, Sergiana! You know Sunshine De Marto has to have a new coat of paint in her dressing room *on the day* of her arrival! And it has to be Whispering Peach!'

'It *is* Whispering Peach!' said Sergiana, sounding like she was going to cry.

'OK, but it's not fresh on this morning! Come on! Get it done again, now!'

Billy heard a door slam. Then the sound of Sergiana, sobbing. And *then* the sound of her (although he wasn't *sure* it was this) opening the lid of a tin of paint.

CHAPTER 33
NOT MY PROBLEM

Hearing this conversation next door left Billy thinking hard. Clearly Sunshine expected the very highest standards in famousness. Clearly Sunshine couldn't meet anyone unless they themselves carried themselves like a very big star indeed. So he called for Styliszts himself – Sergiana was covered in Whispering Peach, but otherwise ready to work – and said:

'Never mind the dressing room. Make *me* look

good. Make *me* Sunshine De Marto ready!'

'Um . . . now?' said Sergio. 'She's going to be here quite soon.'

'Now!' said Billy, tapping his wrist, as if there was a watch on there, which there wasn't.

So they did. This time, Sergio *really* crazied up Billy's hair. By the end of it, there was so much Monkey Snot in there it was like a chimp with hay fever had sneezed on to his head. Sergio shaped and clumped the hair/snot into something that looked a bit like a cross between a hedgehog and a birthday cake that had melted after being set on fire by its own candles. Sergiana didn't quite know what to do to his clothes, beyond the usual thing of adding some accessories to his school uniform, but Billy had some ideas.

'Paint one!'

'What?' said Sergiana.

'Paint one of my school uniforms Whispering Peach!'

'Um . . . are you sure?'

Billy sighed. 'Please don't question me, Sergiana. I don't think that's your job, is it? Your job is to dress me. AS I WISH TO BE DRESSED!'

'Right. Sorry!' said Sergiana. She rushed next door, got the paint pot and a brush, and started slapping it on to the nearest hanging uniform.

'Also, wings.'

'Pardon?'

'I want wings.'

'I could speak to catering . . . ?' said Sergio.

'No! Not chicken wings! *Angel* wings! On the back!'

'Um . . . where are we going to get those? In the next hour?' said Sergiana.

'THAT, SERGIANA, IS NOT MY PROBLEM!' said Billy, and turned his back.

Seconds later, she'd ripped down the white curtains, and he could hear the sounds of snipping and sewing.

CHAPTER 34

M'WAH!
M'WAH!

The audience were in. Even from his dressing room, Billy could hear, through a speaker on the wall, lots of boys and girls and men and women talking and milling around and getting drinks and laughing. The sound of a thousand people, excited. To see him!

Sergio's phone rang. It was Stuart. He said just two words.

'She's here.'

Then he rang off and rang back, and said some more words.

'Bring Billy into her dressing room. She wants to meet him.'

'Will do,' said Sergio, and he clicked off. He looked at Billy. Billy rose. He took a deep breath. He nodded to Sergiana. She approached him from the back, with his remodelled blazer. He put it on. The outfit, with the paint drying on it, was, it has to be said, a little stiff. Plus, the wings, which Sergiana had managed to make beautifully out of the white curtains, pulled on his shoulders a bit.

'What do you think?' he said.

There was a pause. Sergio coughed. Sergiana hummed a little bit of a song that didn't appear to have an actual tune.

'I SAID—'

'INCREDIBLE!' they both said together.

'Good,' said Billy. 'Thought so. One final touch.

Sunglasses, please, Sergiana.'

'But . . . it's already really dark in here.'

'Even with the curtains taken down,' said Sergio.

Billy stared at them. 'What kind of stylists think it's stupid to wear dark glasses indoors?'

'Fair point, actually,' said Sergiana, handing him a pair.

Billy put them on. He stood up and turned to the mirror. It *was* quite hard to see himself. But then Sergio and Sergiana said:

'EVEN BETTER!'

So he knew he must look amazing.

A minute later, Billy was standing outside Sunshine De Marto's dressing room. He could smell, even from outside, the strong scent of flowers, and the even stronger scent of a hundred This Smells Like My Back Gardens. He could hear the gentle song of a whale, somewhere near a tropical paradise. And he could also hear the sound of Stuart, saying, 'Sunshine! How do you do it? Every time I see you,

you look more and more cool! M'wah! M'wah!'

'*Woof! Woof!*'

'Ha-ha, I'm not trying to kiss you, Mindy! Or Mandy! Ow, don't bite me!'

Sergio and Sergiana were standing on either side of Billy. Billy nodded, and Sergio knocked on the door.

'Come in!' said Stuart.

Sergio opened the door. And there she was, at last. Sunshine De Marto, in a beautiful gold-and-silver dress, her hair today a deep black, with her two Chiwaapoos on either side of her, looking up at him.

Sunshine De Marto, the most famous young person on the planet, looking at him, Billy Smith, and smiling.

Smiling a lot. Really, really smiling. She was giving him her biggest ever smile. Laughing, in fact. Laughing and pointing at him. And then falling off her chair, and wiping her eyes, and saying, 'Oh my Lord! Oh, sorry! Sorry! That's the funniest thing I've ever seen. Oh dear. I think I may have wee'd myself!'

CHAPTER 35
★ I CAN STILL BE A STAR ★

Billy tried to leave the room with as much dignity as he could muster. Which was quite difficult, as his Whispering Peach-coloured school uniform was so stiff by now he had to move a bit like a robot. Plus, he couldn't see very clearly, as he was wearing dark glasses and the room was only lit by a hundred This Smells Like My Back Gardens. Plus, as he was flailing around looking for the door, one of his wings came into contact with one of the This Smells Like

My Back Gardens, and caught fire.

'Aarrgh!' he shouted. But this was itself drowned out by Sunshine's – and what sounded to him like also Stuart's and the Styliszts' – laughter. Luckily, the wings were made of some kind of material that only smouldered a bit. He grabbed a bottle of Eternal Spring anyway, and managed to pour some gently carbonated water over the smoulder and put it out. Then he ran out, knocking his wings into a wonky shape on the doorframe as he went.

Ten minutes later, he was hiding in the toilet. Even that wasn't easy, as the paint had made his school uniform so dry and hard he couldn't sit down on the seat. When he tried to, his wings banged against the cistern.

Inside the cubicle, tears pricked in his eyes. He could hear people calling his name. Stuart, Sergio, his mum, his dad – all saying, 'Billy! Billy! Where are you?' He didn't know what to do. He didn't want any of them, especially Sunshine, to see that he was upset and crying.

He took a deep breath. Then he remembered something that Astral had told him to do. *Breathe*. It was supposed to help him not be scared. So he did. He took another deep breath. In . . . and out. In . . . and out. It wasn't that easy, what with it being a tiny bit smelly in the toilet, but he kept going.

As he breathed, he remembered some other things that Astral had intoned during that session. *Believe in yourself . . . Don't care what others are saying about you. You have the power within you. You can do anything!*

And there was one more. Oh, what was it?

Suddenly he heard a different voice from

outside, one coming from the speaker that he had heard the audience milling about on earlier.

'A minute to show. A minute to show. Please could Billy Smith come to the stage.'

He had planned – in as much as he had a plan – not to go on stage any more. He had planned – in as much as he had a plan – just to carry on hiding in the toilet. But now, as he breathed and thought about the words Astral had said, he wasn't sure about that plan. *Maybe*, he thought, *I can still do this. Maybe it doesn't matter what Sunshine De Marto or anyone else thinks. Maybe I can still go on. I can still have my moment. I can still be a* star.

If only I could remember that last thing Astral said. What was it?

Then it came to him.

Ridicule is nothing to be scared of.

He burst out of the toilet and headed for the stage.

CHAPTER 36
WAVE YOUR HANDS IN THE AIR

Somehow, Billy found his way to the side of the stage. From the wings, he could see – although they couldn't see him – the audience. They were definitely excited. The buzz of all of their murmurings had got louder. He could even hear a few of them whispering the word 'Billy'. Some were craning their necks to see the stage better.

Suddenly, the lights went down. The banging theme tune to *In Yer Face!* started up. Really, really loud. Lights whirled around the stage, different colours – red, green, blue, pink, orange and white. Then Jez and Shola came on, dancing to the music. The audience went crazy, cheering and clapping and whooping. Jez and Shola twirled and twerked around, and then stopped and turned to face the audience. They spoke into long silver microphones.

'HELLO, CLUBABILITY!' they shouted.

A huge roar went up from the crowd.

'ARE YOU HAVING A GOOD TIME?' shouted Jez.

Another roar from the crowd, in which you could make out that they were all saying 'YES!' It crossed Billy's mind that this was a bit odd, seeing as nothing much had happened yet, but, then again, every time he had seen a crowd ask this question, that was always how they replied. They never went, all together, 'UM . . . NO, NOT REALLY!'

Meanwhile, Jez and Shola stepped back gracefully, and hoisted themselves backwards on to their high stools. Billy felt suddenly nervous. He wasn't sure he was going to be able to get on the stool. It had been difficult enough in the rehearsal – because it was designed for an adult not an eleven-year-old – but now, in his paint-dried uniform and wings and dark glasses, it was going to be five times as difficult! He tried to focus on Astral's words, about how you could do anything if you believed in yourself. He *would* get on the stool! He would *not* fall off because he was too small and his trousers felt like they were made of cardboard! His wings would *not* fall off or bump Jez and Shola on the head!

But it wasn't working. He could feel himself starting to panic.

'You lucky, lucky people! Have we got a treat for you tonight!' said Jez.

'It's the big one tonight! The hottest of the hot!' said Shola.

'In years to come, you'll be telling your children

that you were there, the night Clubability had a personal appearance from . . .'

Billy closed his eyes. He felt so nervous. He put his hands out in front of him, almost as if reaching for someone – someone who would know what to do. Someone like . . . Sunshine. *If only Sunshine were here, taking my hand,* he thought. *Leading me onstage.*

'You know who!' said Shola. 'He's waiting for us now in the wings!

'Give it up, wave your hands in the air, shout and scream and generally GO WILD for . . .'

And then, just before they said his name, Billy Smith felt a soft hand being placed in his, pulling him along.

CHAPTER 37
DARK GLASSES

He could hear the music. He could hear the applause. He could hear Jez and Shola dancing.

But he wasn't being pulled onstage. He was being pulled *away* from the stage.

That's a bit confusing, he thought. *I thought Sunshine was going to lead me on to the stage and help me on to the stool and then everything was going to be all right.*

But she seemed to be leading him to an exit door, at the side of the building.

That's OK, he thought. *It's* Sunshine. *She knows how to be famous. She knows how to make — or not make — an entrance. She's just taking me away to build up the tension. She knows best.*

So he just followed her, through that exit door. To the outside, where although it was evening, it was still light enough for him to see properly, at last, through his dark glasses.

And to see, as she let go of his hand and turned round to face him, that it wasn't Sunshine De Marto.

It was Bo.

CHAPTER 38
BUT I AM

'**W**hat are you doing!' shouted Billy. 'Are you out of your mind! I need to be onstage! I can hear my entrance music! I can hear my audience! My *people*!'

Billy turned back to the door. It had a big metal handle on it, which he pulled at wildly, putting his feet on it and leaning backwards and everything. It didn't budge.

'Billy,' said Bo.

'Shut up!' He carried on pulling.

'Billy,' said Bo, coming over. 'It's a fire door. An emergency door. It doesn't open from the outside.'

'It does. It has to!' shouted Billy.

'Well, it doesn't,' said Bo. She gently took his hand again. Billy brushed it away. Bo took hold of it again anyway.

Billy turned towards her. 'Why have you done this to me?'

Bo paused. She looked at him. She took out her phone. She held it up and took a photo. Even in the midst of his crossness, even while he was thinking: *Bit of an odd time to want a pic of me*, Billy tried to do a cool starry pose, crossing his arms and leaning back.

'I was in the audience,' she said, looking down at the phone. 'Me and Rinor came. Stuart may have kicked me out of Hashtag Team Billy, but he couldn't stop me buying tickets – although I feel you should pay me back for that at some point. *Nine ninety-nine?* To see my friend from school wave at people?'

'Have you quite finished?'

'No,' she said. 'Look at this.'

She held her phone towards him. Billy squinted. He could see himself, in his Whispering Peach Bracket Wood school uniform (now looking, it has to be said, less Whispering Peach and more Mumbling Rotten Mango) and his wings, which were so wonky and falling apart and dirty they looked like a drowned duck's (not sure a duck can drown, but you take

the point) and his badly Monkey-Snotted hair, and indeed badly Monkey-Snotted face, because much of it seemed to have run down on to his forehead and down the sides by his ears – and his really, he realised now, *far* too big and also wonky dark glasses – and a tiny part of him knew exactly what she meant. But another part of him – the part that was too proud to admit he knew that – said:

'What about it?'

'Come on, Billy. It's me. *Bo*. I saw you like that waiting to go on, and I thought: OK. *Time to stage an intervention.*'

'There wasn't going to be one of those. The show was only ten minutes long!'

'Not an *interval*! An *intervention*. It means when people –' and here, her eyes became moist – 'see someone they really care about doing something stupid, something that might make other people laugh and jeer at them, and they decide to say: "Stop!

Please stop. This isn't good for you. This isn't *you*."'

Billy looked at her. She was crying properly. He felt his heart twitch. But he wasn't sure he was quite ready to give up, and melt, and be nice to her. He still felt angry, and proud. Then he heard, from inside:

'BI-LLY! BI-LLY! BI-LLY!'

It was the crowd chanting his name. It was his audience. Wanting him. Wanting to see *him*. Not Bo. Which fired him up again to think he was right about everything.

So he turned to her and said:

'How *dare* you say I was doing something stupid! Yes, I may look a bit different to normal, and yes, I'm behaving a bit different to normal, but . . . but . . . you're *allowed* to do all that when you're famous! That's what people expect! That's what people *want*! And so I'm going to go round the front, and find my way back to the stage, and I'm going to do my personal appearance like I was supposed to and like my audience are waiting for! Because . . .' he said, drawing himself up to his full height, with some cracking of the very dry paint on his trousers and blazer, 'YOU DON'T KNOW ANYTHING ABOUT IT. BECAUSE YOU AREN'T FAMOUS!'

'Maybe not,' said a voice. 'But I am.'

They turned round. Standing near the building, looking at them, like she'd been there for some time, was Sunshine De Marto.

CHAPTER 39
GERALD

'Um . . . hello . . .' said Billy. Which felt a bit weak, after all his shouting. And also a bit weak, in terms of finally saying something to Sunshine after all this time of not meeting her. But he didn't know what else to say.

'Hello,' said Sunshine. She came closer to him. She smiled. This close to her, Billy felt astounded by how beautiful she was. He was glad he had dark glasses on. It was like staring into the sun.

'Listen,' she carried on, when he didn't say anything, 'I just wanted to say how sorry I am. About laughing. When you came into my dressing room. Sorry. That was really bad.'

'Oh,' said Billy. 'OK.'

'But you do look funny. I mean: hilarious.'

Billy frowned. 'Um . . .'

'So here's the thing. You're actually right, Billy. Famous people *are* allowed to get away with a lot. They are particularly allowed to wear . . .' she looked him up and down, 'um . . . *interesting* clothes and have, um, *interesting* hair. And people won't laugh, no – they'll say stuff like, "Oh, famous person X is setting a whole new style here!" and "Only celebrity Y could carry off these trousers!" But the thing is, Billy, I don't think that's the kind of fame you have. I think what people like about you is that—'

'I'm so ordinary,' said Billy. He didn't say it with much enthusiasm.

'Well,' said Sunshine, 'yeah. Kind of. And I think Bo . . . it's Bo, right?'

'Yes!' said Bo, who Billy could tell was also very excited to meet Sunshine – and now very excited that Sunshine knew her name – but was trying to contain it.

'I think Bo is right that people out there might laugh at you.'

'But that doesn't matter! Does it? Astral said, "Ridicule is nothing to be scared of."'

'Astral? Don't listen to that clown. For a start, his real name is Gerald.'

'It is?'

'Billy,' said Sunshine, 'let me tell you something. The weird thing about fame is: people you've never met, they think they love you. They seem to *really* love you. But they don't know *you* at all. And so it's . . . dangerous. Because, if you become something that they think isn't what they want you to be, they get . . .

well, kind of angry. They feel disappointed. And then they can turn on you. And it can be horrible. Very horrible.'

There was a silence after she said this. Although they could still hear the distant sound of the audience chanting, 'BI-LLY! BI-LLY!' But it was getting fainter. Like fewer and fewer people were doing it. Like some of the audience were just leaving. And you could also hear Jez saying, 'Sorry, is he coming on or what?'

'Has that,' said Bo, 'happened to you?'

Sunshine shook her head, her black hair swaying from side to side across her face.

'No. Not yet. But it's happened to some people I know. And –' she looked, for a second, sad – 'it *will* happen to me.'

Billy and Bo exchanged glances. Billy took off his dark glasses. And said:

'So . . . what should I do?'

Sunshine shrugged. 'Well, I think let's get you back to your dressing room – change you back to your normal clothes – and then you go out there and be just normal – ordinary Billy Smith – and let's do the show!'

'But . . . there'll be no one left by the time I go on?'

Sunshine smiled. 'That's not true. There won't be *so many* people. But the ones who stay? They'll be the *real* fans. The ones who accept you however you are.'

Billy thought about this for a second. Then he looked at Bo.

Bo nodded. And smiled.

'OK,' said Billy.

CHAPTER 40
NOT THE CHRISTMAS PLAY

Billy was right. There weren't that many people left in the audience by the time they got him back to the dressing room, and into his normal clothes, and sorted out his hair, and back to the side of the stage.

Where they bumped into Stuart. He was wearing a microphone on the side of his face. And, for once, he was really *not* smiling.

'BILLY! WHERE HAVE YOU BEEN? THIS EVENT HAS BEEN RUINED! RUINED! DO YOU KNOW

HOW MUCH IT COST! OF COURSE YOU DON'T, YOU STUPID LITTLE BOY! IT'S ALL BEEN A WASTE OF TIME!'

'Um . . .' said Billy, 'I . . .'

'Don't shout at him!' said Bo. 'He's Billy Smith!' She put his arm round him. 'The *famous* Billy Smith!'

Billy looked at her. He felt, in his normal clothes, and his normal hair, suddenly incredibly touched that she said that.

Stuart only stared at Bo, though.

'OMG! WHAT ARE YOU DOING HERE!' he said eventually. He started talking into his head mic. 'Security. Security. Unwanted person in the building. Please come to the side of the stage.'

A hand appeared, and took the microphone away from his face. And then snapped it, with a crack, in two.

'WHAAA—' said Stuart, before looking round,

and seeing that the hand doing the cracking was Sunshine De Marto's.

'Oh,' he said. 'Hello.' He moved his face towards her, and pursed his lips, as if about to kiss her on the cheek. She backed away.

'Don't do that, Stuart. I hate it when you go "M'wah! M'wah!" on my cheeks. It's not even a proper kiss. I think maybe you just do it to make that stupid noise.'

'Oh. Sorry.'

'So. Re Hashtag Billy.'

'Right, yes. Of course. What's your thinking?'

'Billy had a little rethink about how to do this gig,' said Sunshine. 'He needed to take a little time out to do that, with me, and Bo. But we're sorted now. And ready.'

'Right,' said Stuart, whose whole attitude, especially all his crossness, had changed since Sunshine appeared, and he was now nodding a lot and smiling again. 'Um, just one thing. Might be better maybe to postpone to another time. You know. Do the whole thing again. As –' he craned his neck so he could get a view of the audience – 'it's not quite as heaving out there as it was.'

Billy and Bo and Sunshine looked out. Stuart was right. In terms of Sunshine's point, though – about how when you're famous, the people who think they know you don't really know you – well, this particular audience was mainly people who *did* actually know Billy. His mum, his dad and his baby sister Lisa; Rinor; Dan, Natasha and Suz; Mr Carter, Miss Gerard and a few more boys and girls from his class at Bracket Wood – they were the people who had stayed on. Everyone else had left. And, in fairness, baby Lisa didn't even have a choice – she was strapped into her sling.

Billy looked at the very few people remaining. They looked less like an audience who were excited, less of a charged-up-and-waiting-with-bated-breath-for-their-idol-to-emerge audience, and more like a bored one that was maybe waiting for the school play to start. And not the Christmas play, when the assembly hall would normally be full. No. A play about school life that Miss Gerard had staged on a Wednesday evening that only the die-hards turned up to.

'I mean . . . even Jez and Shola have gone,' observed Stuart. 'So – obviously you know best, Sunshine – but I *really* think maybe we should reschedule.'

Sunshine looked at Billy.

'What do you think?'

'Um . . . well, I was going to ask *you* that,' he said.

'Because you think I know all about being onstage and stuff? I know. But *you* are Billy Smith and you're famous yourself now, so maybe – just by maybe taking into account what I said outside about how, when you're famous, most people don't know who you are, but there are always going to be some people who do – people who know *exactly* who you are . . . and maybe they're the ones who really matter . . . So maybe you should make up your own mind on that.'

Billy thought about what she'd said. He looked around for Bo, but she seemed to have vanished.

Then he looked to Stuart, and said:

'Play my entrance music!'

And he walked onstage.

But there wasn't any entrance music, as the guy who had been ready to cue that up had also gone home.

CHAPTER 41
WHO YOUR REAL FRIENDS ARE

Billy Smith's personal appearance at Clubability was, then, more . . . low key than had been planned. But it was also really *nice*.

It ended up just being him and Sunshine sitting on the high stools – she helped him, carefully, to get on his – and having a chat. *She* interviewed *him*! Which was also not what Billy had expected. She asked him lots of questions about what his life had been like since

School Daze started, and Billy answered, saying some of it had been really fun, and some of it had been kind of weird. And then he told some stories about what had happened to him, and she laughed a lot, especially when he admitted that he'd been trying to meet her for ages, but that every time he went to any celebrity thing she just seemed to be leaving by the other door.

The audience, small though it was, seemed to really enjoy it too. Some of them – especially once they realised Sunshine was part of the show – were recording it on their phones. Others were laughing and clapping a lot. The sound of this, it has to be said, was not overwhelming. But the feeling in the room was that everybody did really love Billy. Except possibly Mr Carter and Miss Gerard. But they did seem to genuinely like him.

One bit everyone seemed to particularly like was when Sunshine said: 'Is there anything you feel you've learned from your brush with fame, Billy?'

Billy thought for a minute, then said:

'Yes. I think I've learned that, although it can be really fun, it can make you forget stuff.' He frowned. 'I don't mean like where you live, or where you left your keys . . .'

'Right. No.'

'I mean, like, important stuff. Like who you really are. And who your real friends are. On which note . . .'

'Yes . . . ?'

'I'd like to invite someone else up onstage, if that's OK?'

Sunshine smiled. 'Sure, Billy. Don't forget: it's *your* stage.'

Billy nodded. He looked out into the audience,

squinting against the spotlight.

'Bo? Are you still here?'

There was a short pause. And then her voice came out of the darkness: 'Yeah?'

'Do you mind – I mean, would you like to come up here for a bit?'

There was another short pause.

Eventually the answer came back: 'Not sure.'

Billy looked at Sunshine. Sunshine laughed.

'Maybe you need to say something more to get your friend up here?' she said.

Billy thought for a second, then nodded.

'I guess the reason I'd like you to come up, Bo, is that I've realised something. Which I didn't realise before. And that is: you're not just my best friend. It's that all the time this fame thing was happening to me, you were doing what best friends are supposed to do. *You were looking out for me*. You were trying to protect me. From Stuart.

From the trolls. And . . .' He stopped for a second, and peered more deeply into the light. 'From myself.'

The audience was hushed. Not just quiet: hushed. No one, as it happens, was holding a pin above the ground, but had they been doing so you could have heard it drop.

'So what I'm saying is,' Billy continued, 'I'm sorry. I'm sorry I didn't see any of that while it was happening. And so I was stupid and horrible to you. So, yes – sorry. And . . . thank you.'

Billy had said all this looking straight out towards the audience. So he couldn't see something. Which is that, while he was talking, Bo had walked round the side of the stage and come to stand next to his stool.

'That's OK,' she said, smiling. 'I forgive you.'

Everyone in the crowd burst into spontaneous applause.

Suz even took out her enormous phone, clicked on a page and deleted the words 'Work on Billy's apologising skills'.

CHAPTER 42
★ FISH FINGERS, CHIPS AND PEAS ★

The applause continued for a while. Bo did a little bow to the audience, and then went off.

Sunshine said, 'Wow. Amazing. That was beautiful, Billy! I don't think we can top that. So maybe it's time to end the night, and—'

'Um . . . Sunshine . . .' said Billy.

'Yes?'

'Sorry, I know you're wrapping everything up, but I just wanted to say . . . you're not like I expected.'

'In what way?'

'Um . . . you know . . . with the candles, and the lighting, and the whale music, and the temperature control, and having loads of people around you doing stuff all the time, and Stuart saying you can't even meet Bo because everyone on Hashtag Team Billy has to be exactly right for you to meet them . . . I thought you'd be more . . .'

'Into being famous?'

'Well, yes.'

She laughed. 'Stuart *tells* everyone I need all that stuff. He says –' she added, doing a brilliant impression of Stuart – 'that it "keeps Hashtag Team Sunshine on their toes, and makes them *think* you're a star, darling!" But once I actually meet people properly I tell them not to bother.'

'OK!' said Stuart, suddenly appearing from the audience and trying to climb up on to the stage. 'That's enough! It was bad enough when that . . . girl came on and we had that grisly apology – which, by the way, almost definitely contained a libel against me and TOTALTV TV . . .' As he said this, Stuart was trying again and again to get on to the stage, but each time he lifted his body up it just slid back down again. 'But now it's definitely . . . ugh . . .' he said, trying to push himself up again, and failing again, 'time for this show to end! We have a curfew! We have insurance issues! Goodnight!'

'He says it's all about my *brand*,' continued Sunshine, as if Stuart wasn't there, at her feet, trying to climb up. 'Ugh. How I hate that word. And my brand is supposed to be glamorous and exciting and extraordinary. But I'm not really. I hate it sometimes, having to pretend to be. Like, I have to eat all this silly posh food. And post photos of me eating that stuff on Instagram and whatnot. But I mainly like—'

'NO!' shouted Stuart, from the bottom of the stage. 'DON'T SAY IT! PEOPLE ARE RECORDING

THIS ON THEIR PHONES!'

'FISH FINGERS, CHIPS AND PEAS!' shouted Sunshine.

The whole audience applauded and cheered. Then Billy raised his hands, and with confidence – with the confidence of someone who did actually know a bit now about being a star – said:

'HEY, CLUBABILITY! GIVE IT UP FOR FISH FINGERS, CHIPS AND PEAS!'

And the whole audience shouted back: 'FISH FINGERS, CHIPS AND PEAS!'

'SUNSHINE DE MARTO LOVES FISH FINGERS, CHIPS AND PEAS!' shouted Billy.

With a huge effort, Stuart leaped up on to the stage and tried to get in the way of Sunshine, who was waving her hands in the air crying, 'I DO! I DO! ESPECIALLY WITH BROWN SAUCE.'

Unfortunately, as Stuart made his leap, his very tight black trousers split at the back. More

unfortunately, this coincided with Sunshine shouting the words 'BROWN SAUCE!'

Even *more* unfortunately, that meant the audience started pointing and laughing at his exposed baggy-grey-panted bum.

Even *more* and *more* unfortunately, Mindy and Mandy ran on at that point from the side of the stage, yapping and trying to bite his exposed grey-panted bum.

Which meant that he had to run offstage holding his hands over it. And leave Billy Smith and Sunshine De Marto and the audience singing and shouting madly about fish fingers, chips and peas.

CHAPTER 43
MINCED FRIED HAND-PARTS FROM THE MARINE KINGDOM

'**F**ish fingers, chips and peas!' said Jane Smith, bringing out, on a tray, six plates of the said delicacy. She put the tray down on their dinner table, and started handing round the plates.

'Brilliant!' said Billy. 'Where's the brown sauce?'

'I love brown sauce!' said Rinor, who was joining them for tea. 'Although in Balmadömölk we call it *Brunnsmerznadelmusstardin Dann Schnick-Schnick!*'

'What does that mean?'

'Brown sauce!' said Rinor, as if it was obvious.

'Aha!' said Billy's dad. 'It *was* here! I made it disappear!'

'What, under the table?' said Bo, who was also there, looking under the table.

'Dad!' said Billy. 'Stuart told you not to do that! It's against our brand! Our ordinary brand!'

'Yes,' said John, 'but Stuart – and his cameras – aren't here any more, are they!'

They weren't. Filming on *At Home with the Ordinarys* had not continued. After a chat with his mum and dad, Billy had decided having a TV crew in their house filming their every move wasn't something he wanted any more, especially if – which he now sensed they did not – his parents didn't want it either.

He'd been to see Stuart at TOTALTV TV, and told him. He'd thought that Stuart would shout a lot, and bring out the contract. He did bring out the contract. But he said:

'To be honest with you, Billy, since the personal appearance went so pear-shaped, no one's that interested in you any more anyway. So . . .' And he tore the contract up. And then turned his back.

Billy shrugged, although not before noticing that Stuart's trousers seemed to have a new . . . *layer* sewn into the back, to make sure they didn't split again.

'No,' said Billy now, to his dad. 'The cameras are definitely gone. Ah well. It was fun while it lasted . . .'

'And things *are* a bit different from what they were,' said Jane. 'I mean, we don't always have a superstar for tea!'

'Ha!' said Sunshine, tucking into her second fish finger, dunked heavily in brown sauce. By her feet, Mindy and Mandy were gobbling up some leftovers. 'Do you mean me or Billy, Mrs Smith?'

'Um . . .'

'Or yourself! Because I think of *you* as a bit of a superstar!'

Jane Smith blushed, but also beamed. 'Don't be so silly, Sunshine!'

Yes, Sunshine De Marto – despite her massive number of followers across all platforms, and despite her closely guarded brand of only ever existing in an extra-special world of fine food and yachts and VIP areas – was having fish fingers, chips and peas at Billy Smith's house. Billy, to be honest, still had to pinch himself to believe it. But she was clearly enjoying herself. And his parents and Bo and Rinor were clearly enjoying that she was there. Even the baby, in her high seat at the corner of the table, seemed to be gurgling happily and smiling on seeing her.

'Still, Billy . . .' Bo said. 'Are you OK? You know. Now that it's kind of . . . over?'

'Never say that to a famous person, Bo,' said Sunshine. 'Remember: there's always the shopping channels.'

Billy laughed. 'I don't know, Bo. I think

I'm fine with it. I think, at the end of the day, I am . . . ordinary. And I'm quite happy being ordinary.'

Sunshine, who had – again, against the brand a bit – wolfed her food down, started to get up. Her phone was bleeping a lot.

'Sorry, guys,' she said, looking at the notifications that were pinging up on the screen. 'I think I may have to go. Thanks so much for tea!'

'That's OK, Sunshine!' said John.

'Yes, come back soon!' said Jane.

Sunshine was putting her coat on. It was a very white one that looked like it was made of feathers. It went with her hair, which today was completely white.

'Thank you. I will!' she said. 'Mindy! Mandy! Come!' Then, just before she left, she went over to Billy, still seated at the table, and crouched down next to him.

'You're not ordinary, Billy. Do you know why? Because you are really, really nice. And that . . . is extraordinary!' And she kissed him gently on the cheek.

Billy went very red. And said, softly: 'Thank you.'

'By-eee!' Sunshine said, getting up and waving. She went out of the room. From inside the room, they could still hear her phone bleeping.

'More fish fingers, Bill?' said Jane.

'No thanks, Mum,' said Billy.

'John?'

'No thanks, Mum,' said John.

'Bo?'

'No thank you, Mrs Smith.'

'Rinor?'

'Yes, please. In Balmadömölk, we call them *Vorsh Mol Nih Shomly Boteache!*'

'I assume that just means fish fingers,' said Bo.

'No, it means Minced Fried Hand-Parts from the Marine Kingdom.'

'Oh.'

Mrs Smith went out into the kitchen to get some more tea.

Billy took a deep breath. He could feel how everything was returning to normal: to the quiet, unstressful, ordinary life he was used to.

'Mum,' he said, loud enough for her to hear in the kitchen. 'How about I look after Lisa tonight? Like

I was going to ages ago? You and Dad could have some proper time on your own.'

'That would be lovely, Billy,' said Jane, coming back through the door. 'What do you say, John?'

'Um . . . I may need to run it past Steve, Dave and Mike from the other office,' said Billy's dad.

'Are you joking?'

'Yes.'

'I've told you never to try that.' She turned back to Billy. 'Are you sure?'

'Of course.' He turned to Bo and Rinor. 'Actually, guys – I was thinking – I've got the DVD of *Ratatouille* waiting to go. You could stay here tonight and watch it with me maybe, if your parents say it's OK?'

'I'll call my mum now!' said Bo.

'Can you get her to ask my mum?' said Rinor.

'Sure!' said Bo.

'Tell her to tell my mum I'll join the Zoom call to the Great-Uncle Erag and the cousins later.'

'You have Zoom in Balmadömölk?' said Bo.

'Please, Bo. It's a very modern place. Of course.' Rinor paused. 'Although it's a slightly different software whose name translates as "Fasty Goings from One Place to Another on the Talky-Talky Box".'

Everyone laughed, not least at the possibility that Rinor had perhaps always just been making stuff up about his homeland.

Billy smiled, looking at his lovely friends, his lovely parents and his lovely baby sister, Lisa, who was trying to eat a plastic spoon.

Yes, life is ordinary again, he thought. *And that's good* . . . even though being famous – being extraordinary – had been fun while it lasted.

And then, suddenly, Sunshine burst back in.

'**O**MG! Billy!' she said. 'You know my phone's been going a lot?'

'Yes?'

'Well, someone's put a vid of me and you leading the crowd singing "Fish Fingers, Chips and Peas!" on YouTube! And it's got . . . six million views!' She looked down. 'Oops. Eight million now!'

'Oh,' said Billy. 'Is that bad? Won't Stuart be cross I've spoiled your brand?'

'Never mind him!' she said. 'It's great! People love it! Prinze Noize wants me and you to do it as a rap! And then maybe do a whole album based on it! There's even talk of a food show on TV called it, starring you and me.' She laughed a lot, and then said to Billy: 'Whaddayasay?'

And I wonder what Billy did say . . .

Thanks to:

My eternal thanks for help making this book happen go as ever to my illustrator Steven Lenton and to everyone I work with at HarperCollins, notably Ann-Janine Murtagh, Nick Lake, Sam Stewart, Elorine Grant, Kate Clarke, Tanya Hougham and Sam White.

And also, Georgia Garrett at RCW, Mary-Grace Brunker at Avalon, and, for this one, the good ship Showbiz in which I have sailed, sometimes rockily, for many years.